D1011359

THE HIGH ROAD

BOOKS BY FAITH BALDWIN

Arizona Star

The Moon's Our Home

The Office Wife

Station Wagon Set

Twenty Four Hours a Day

Change of Heart

Garden Oats

The High Road

Hotel Hostess

Letty and the Law

Men are such Fools

Rehersal for Love

That Man is Mine

White-Collar Girl

White Magic

FAITH BALDWIN

THE

HIGH

ROAD

AEONIAN PRESS, INC.
NEW YORK, N.Y.
1974

TO

JULIE EIDESHEIM

in admiration and gratitude . . .
just one of the many books which would
never see print were it not for her thankless
job of Governess to Brain Children.

THE HIGH ROAD

CHAPTER I

JILL sat cross-legged on the studio divan and contemplated her shoes. They were small shoes, and had once been sturdy. They were scuffed, they were run down at the heels, and there was a hole in the sole of the left one. They had been tapped, half-soled, renovated once too often. For months they had been a brave and polished black but just at present the polish wouldn't take. Jill looked from the shoes to the ink bottle in her hand. A spot of ink here, a spot of ink there? No, really, it wouldn't do at all. Ink had a way of turning blue by daylight.

She set the shoes and the ink bottle on the uneven floor. She chuckled and pushed the wild red hair back from her pale and pointed face. A cracked mirror over the bureau facing her gave her back her reflection. Others, she thought, might be down to their last yacht, but thank heaven she still had two practically untouched lipsticks.

She yawned and stretched and the sagging springs creaked. Jill was light as a feather, slim as a willow

3

wand, but even small good bones weigh a little and the divan had seen much better days. A mere one hundred and five pounds was too great a burden.

A wild spring rain lashed at the windows. Not a nice, straight-falling rain at all, but one informed with fury, and blowing from the four corners of the earth. It would be wet and puddly underfoot and new shoes were certainly indicated. She'd lost her rubbers. Well, should it be rubbers and a bright new hat, or good shoes and no rubbers and no hat?

Jill slid off the couch and went over to the window. It was dusk and the street lights were on, yellow in the rain. The asphalt was a shining black. . . . A very cheerless outlook.

Jill wore a tweed skirt, very well cut, a leftover which had served its time. It was marvelous, she reflected, what a beating a really good tweed would take and still retain its original lines. She wore also a very pretty pull-over which she had bought for so little that time in Bermuda. Thinking of Bermuda, Jill giggled irrepressibly. The winter before last she had chaperoned the Terrible Twins to the Island, and delivered them safely to their platinum-blond, alimonied mother. The Twins had constituted one job which always gave her pleasure in retrospect . . . the trip to Bermuda, a two days' holiday there, and then back, all expenses paid and fifty dollars over. Moreover, she had

4

won a pool and augmented her income by fifty more. She had had a sea tan, a new beau—the purser, very brass-buttoned and correct—and the pull-over to show for it. She had also acquired a very sore pair of shins, because when Harold wasn't kicking her, Gwendolyn was.

Fun, just the same. People on board, before reading the passenger list, had assumed that she was the mother of the twins— "I wonder if she's a widow or divorced . . . she looks so young, poor child!"—but when they found out a little later that she wasn't the mother at all, but a hired hand, they had been even nicer to her, realizing that she was not to blame for the twins' extraordinary lack of upbringing.

Jill went over to the bureau and ran a comb through her coppery waves, pressing them back into shape. She grinned at herself in the glass. She looked, she decided, underfed but interesting. Well, it wasn't the first time she had been out of a job. In the seven years which had elapsed since her arrival in New York she had held perhaps two dozen positions with varying intervals between them.

She had long eyes, surprisingly slanted at the corners, a bright, wicked hazel with more than a suggestion of green. She had high cheekbones, a pointed chin, a mobile mouth, and a pert nose. She had slender limbs, and a round little waist, and she didn't look twenty-five years old. She looked, in the tweed and pull-over, about fourteen.

She found a dime on the bureau, tossed it in mid-air, slapped it smartly on the back of her hand. Rubbers and a hat, then. She knew the very hat. It had verve. It said something to the beholder. It was in reduced circumstances just as she was, being a smart, leftover Palm Beach felt with a tricky brim. No straw for her, here today and gone tomorrow. Perhaps people would look at the hat and forget the shoes.

Mrs. Larsen, her landlady, plodded to the foot of the stairs and howled up, three flights,

"Gentleman to see you, Miss Hamilton."

That would be Jimmy. Jill crossed the small room and went out to the uncarpeted corridor, leaned perilously over the stair well and howled back. "Tell him I'll be right down."

Mrs. Larsen was conventional. She maintained a brownstone lodging house on the East Side, on a street as yet unfashionable, and she exacted rent in advance, no cooking in the rooms, and no gentlemen callers. Otherwise she was a good egg. When Jill had had the awful cold, after returning from the South American trip, on which she had officiated as hostess, Mrs. Larsen had daily and nightly ascended the stairs with broth, aspirin, and good advice.

Jill powdered her nose, applied the brighter of the

lipsticks, pulled an old felt hat over her spectacular hair at the best possible angle, seized an umbrella which had suffered recently from crushed ribs, shrugged herself into a raincoat, and galloped downstairs. She didn't lock the door after her. That would have hurt Mrs. Larsen's feelings, and moreover she had nothing to steal. She carried her entire fortune with her in a very good alligator bag which had been a gift from a ci-devant employer.

Jimmy Bates was walking around the Larsen drawing room. It was purest early Victorian: flowers, waxen under glass, and chromos; carved rocking chairs. A center table with an electrified oil lamp, the shade of china tastefully decorated in roses; a Brussels carpet, and lace tidies. Jimmy, as Jill entered, inquired plaintively:

"Why does it always smell of cabbage?"

He always asked that, and Jill never answered. It was a hypothetical question. She said, instead:

"It's a dreadful night. I'm not going far. Let's eat at Joe's."

Jimmy put his hand in his pocket and produced a five-dollar bill. "This is on me," he said, "I'm in funds."

"Jimmy, how perfectly swell!"

They looked at each other and laughed. They were very much alike, somehow. Jimmy was slim and sandy, his face was square and his eyes were gray, but there was something in the defiance of their bearing, their almost British carelessness, which proclaimed that each would rather die than express a deep emotion, which allied them.

"Where'd you get it?" demanded Jill, regarding the five-spot as if it were an unnatural phenomenon, a Barnum curiosity.

"I sold something."

"No! What?"

Jimmy "wrote." That is, he wanted to write. He had a decrepit typewriter and between jobs, any sort of jobs, he picked out words on it. He had written a stark Russian tale which Jill thought quite marvelous; a light late Michael Arlen story of the Riviera, unvisited by the author; a very grim little tale of Broadway with a chuckle in the middle, patterned on Mr. Hellinger; and a three-act play in very blank verse.

"Which, Jimmy?" she demanded, and shook him. "Was it 'Sonia' or 'The Duchess Remembers' or—"

Jimmy said sadly, "It was 'Household Hints.' But they paid me."

Jill burst into wild laughter and Jimmy joined her. Mrs. Larsen, ponderously and deliberately passing by, wondered what they had to laugh at, the two of them. Not that it mattered. Jill's rent was paid for a month and Jill was a nice girl, a very nice girl, only, Mrs.

Larsen wondered further, why she didn't go home? Even if she didn't have any near relatives, there must be someone who'd take her in. New York wasn't a place for a girl, not nowadays.

Jill put her arm through Jimmy's and they went out, shut the heavy door behind them, ran down the crumbling wet steps, turned west toward Lexington, where Joe's Italian Cuisine sign, in brightest neon, would presently wink at them from a corner.

Once established at their special table, plentifully supplied with antipasto and awaiting the arrival of the thick and steaming minestrone which, thank heaven, stuck to your lean and hungry ribs, they toasted each other in the red wine which was part of the "Super One-Fifty Dinner" and proceeded to make their reports, as they had not seen each other for several days.

"Any luck, Jill?"

"No. I've been around . . . nothing doing in the cruise line . . . and I tried for a receptionist job but didn't land it. Phillips—that's the photographer on Fifth—I filled in for him once when the regular girl was on a long vacation—was nice enough, but he wants someone who will bring in the cash customers. Someone with a Name and a Circle he said, all in capitals. A lot of photographers are going in for dizzy debutantes who feel they are being in the swim to work but don't demand much in the way of salary

9

and have a lot of friends—can't you just hear 'em on the phone? . . . 'Oh, Babs, darling, I've found the most *divine* photographer—he makes you look like Garbo and Dietrich and Harlow all in one!' "

Jimmy grunted. "Tough!" was all he said.

"Well, I've still hope. I went to see Mrs. Emory."

"Who's she? No, don't tell me, let me guess. Was that the female whose husband had the freak show concession in Coney Island where you sold tickets?"

"Very cold. Positively frigid."

"Was she the old lady you drove to Florida a year or so ago . . . or the one who ran the dress shop down there, where you modeled?"

"Getting warmer. I met Mrs. Emory again in Florida during the season when I was selling—not modeling, Jimmy. I'm too small to do much modeling, you know that. No, she was the old lady to whom I was reader-companion the second year I was in New York. You remember . . . I told you about her place on Long Island and the New York house? Elegant. Out of a novel. Her companion who'd been with her thirty years had a breakdown and went home to England, and I got the temporary place—three months— through an agency. Mrs. Emory was a grand person . . . is, I mean. Well, I went to see her, thought perhaps the companion felt in need of another holiday or something, but nothing doing. She was there, a fixture, tall as Carnera, thin as morning milk, and grim as a ghost story. But Mrs. Emory was swell. Gave me tea and crumpets."

"Today?" cried Jimmy. "Come across! Because with that under your belt if you wangled a dollar-fifty Super Dinner out of me . . . !"

"No, yesterday. And said she'd keep me in mind, she often hears of a place for a girl of my versatility," announced Jill, beaming.

"Does she ever hear of one for a young man, just as versatile, if not as pretty?" inquired Jimmy. "University trained to nothing at all, and doing his best to turn an honest penny."

"I'll ask her next time I see her," Jill promised cheerfully. "Oh, Jimmy, I wish you could get something permanent."

"I do too," he said; "looks like I'm getting old or something."

He was twenty-six. Jill shrugged her shoulders. She said, "Well, it does look as if Youth Would be Served. All the jobs are being grabbed up by the kids—just out of high, or two years of college or business school."

"Sure," agreed Jimmy, and wrapped spaghetti with loving care and technique about his fork, "we were born a little too early or a little too late. Besides, we hadn't the foresight to specialize."

"Dan Hardy says—"

"Wait a minute!" said Jimmy. "I thought it was understood that we weren't to mention Dan Hardy on this expedition."

"I forgot," said Jill, not in the least contritely.

"I'll refresh your memory," Jimmy offered. "Last time we had dinner together—"

"Hot dogs and cokes at the lunch stand," she murmured.

"Well, dogs and cokes at the lunch stand," he amended, "you Dan-Hardyed me this and Dan-Hardyed me that until I was fed to the teeth. I got just a little bit tired of hearing about the sterling qualities of the noble young engineer who would rather starve than prostitute his profession. Well, personally I think starving uncomfortable." He looked at her with considerable animosity and then burst out, "Really, Jill, I wish you hadn't landed that South American cruise job. Meeting Hardy aboard unsettled you completely."

"No, it didn't," she denied thoughtfully. She absorbed the last bit of spaghetti, sighed and attacked a limp salad, while the agile waiter with the beaming smile and slightly soiled apron refilled her wineglass, "Only . . . Well, Dan Hardy has a purpose somehow. That means a lot. We've arrived at the place where we haven't any, you and I. He's been knocking about longer than we have but he hasn't been diverted.

12

Every job he has taken as a stopgap has been in some way related to his engineering, even if he could have demanded more money at something else. We've got so that we don't care what the next job is or how long it lasts as long as something turns up."

"You are talking through your hat," said Jimmy simply. "And, by the way, you've a smudge on your nose; said hat crocked off, I take it."

Jill ignored the smudge. She said stubbornly, "But anyway Dan's made me realize that if I could get something steady, something lasting, something with a future—"

"I thought you recovered from that dream years ago," said Jimmy. He waved his salad aside and waited for the spumoni, adding aggrievedly, "It wasn't your fault that you came down here to click on the radio and didn't click, was it? It wasn't mine that my people saw me through college and then couldn't do any more for me owing to well-known circumstances beyond their control? Or that I majored in English Lit, and meant to be a writer, and planned postgrad courses and travel and maybe a publishing house job to get experience."

Jill looked at him, the hazel-green eyes narrowed. She liked him enormously, he was the gayest possible companion. She had known him for three years and there were times when she believed that she was a little

13

in love with him; not too much for comfort, just enough to make their encounters warm and exciting and faintly dangerous. But she liked him better when he wasn't complaining about his lost opportunities, when he was at his most lighthearted and casual. Not that there was anything casual in the occasional kisses. But she wouldn't let that happen often, she didn't dare. She was now and then desperately lonely, and sometimes afraid. Of late the periods of loneliness and fear had lessened, time lengthened between them, and when they did find the chink in her armor and attacked her it was with less intensity. She said hotly:

"Other people have managed to write and have some little old job they didn't like especially on the side. They haven't needed PG courses—or college either, for that matter—or travel. You had the chance in the advertising agency, Jimmy. It was up your alley, I mean, along your lines, and it paid enough to eat and you could write after hours. But you wouldn't stick it."

He said, shrugging, "I couldn't. Of all the eyewash . . . and the things they expected me to do! I was a glorified office boy."

She said evenly, "But you couldn't get to be an ace copy writer in two months, Jimmy."

The last, lingering, melting sweetness of the spu-

14

moni vanished from their spoons. And Jill sighed again, "Boy, if I could get something permanent."

Jimmy laughed, his good humor restored by the final glass of acid red wine. He said, amused:

"Darling, you'd hate it. You were meant to be a bird on the wing; or, if you weren't meant to be, you've adapted yourself nicely. Think of all the fun you've had. Remember the time you answered the phone for the phony stock salesman and found yourself in court? And the ticket selling at Coney Island?" He grinned at her because it was during an off evening that he had subwayed to Coney Island and found Jill valiantly doubling in brass as ticket seller and barker, the barker having taken a drop too much, and sleeping it off in the back room, visited occasionally and wrathfully by the fat lady, who happened to be married to him, and the freak show's irate manager.

"It was fun," she admitted, and smiled back.

The check came, Jimmy paid it, added a lordly tip, and said, as they made their way out of the smoky room between the crowded tables, "The exchequer will run to the movies: double feature, and not more than forty cents. We can do it on less if you'll walk a few blocks."

Jill yawned.

"I'm sleepy," she told him, "and tomorrow I go out job hunting. Save the eighty cents. I'll start answering

15

ads again." She laughed. "That has its points too, besides the wear and tear on shoe leather—and you never know where you'll land."

She remembered briefly the time she had answered a chorus call. Her figure was all right and her face would certainly pass muster and she could sing, far better than the average chorus girl, if not well enough to get by on the radio. But, oddly, she couldn't dance. She always thought she could and certainly on a ball-room floor she was able to acquit herself decently, but it appeared that chorus girls nowadays had to know more than the simpler ballroom steps.

She said, forgetting that fleet humiliation:

"If worst comes to worst I might get another job walking Park Avenue dogs . . . Did I tell you I did that once? Their owner had a maid who objected and a butler who was just too-too above that sort of thing, so I came around three times a day and walked the nasty little brutes. Three of them. That's how I met Hennesy the cop and his fat wife . . . they were swell people . . . I used to go to dinner Sundays with them. The dog job was hard on the feet but it paid, and I think I might have gone on indefinitely if I hadn't happened to hit Fifi—oh, not very hard—in a moment of bitter exasperation. And Fifi's mamma saw; and fired me. If Fifi had bitten me it might have been a break—they'd rather pay up than be sued, you know."

She added, "I told that to Dan Hardy. He said I was Jill of all trades and master of none—"

"Why bring him up again?" asked Jimmy.

He took her back to Mrs. Larsen's. Standing in the doorway with the rain, now a fine cold mist rather than a driving wetness, penetrating their clothes and cold on their faces, he held her hands and tried to draw her toward him. "Come on," he said caressingly, "relax, loosen up, don't be so unkind. You can be so darned sweet."

"But I don't want to be," Jill declared, and drew her hands away. "At least, not now."

She escaped and presently was inside the house, going up the echoing stairs, treading lightly because the front bedroom and parlor on the second floor was occupied by Mrs. Larsen's best paying guest, a very crotchety old lady. She thought, Perhaps it's good that —that I haven't background, haven't a place where I can ask Jimmy to come; perhaps it's just as well that we have to eat at places like Joe's and go to the movies or just stand in a doorway. It's—it's safer.

She was nearly at the top when the telephone rang downstairs and Mrs. Larsen called her. "It's for you, Miss Hamilton."

Jill ran downstairs again. It must be Dan, he had promised to call when he returned to town. She thought, If he wants to come see me . . . ? Oh, surely if Mrs. Larsen isn't having company she'll let us use the parlor and we'll be quiet, it isn't very late, just nine. . . . She thought, I can wear the blue dress he liked so much on board ship.

She had some pretty clothes. She bought them when she could—almost—afford them and saved them for jobs. On hostess jobs you had to dress, and on companion jobs too.

She picked up the instrument dangling from the wall and said breathlessly:

"Hello, Jill Hamilton speaking."

CHAPTER II

DAN's voice answered. He said, "Jill? This is Dan. I got in a few hours ago. Is it too late to come see you?"

"No," Jill answered, "it isn't. It's just the right time. Fact is, I only came in a minute or so ago myself."

"I'll be along," said Dan.

Jill replaced the instrument and looked at the dingy brown wallpaper covered with sprawling faded yellow flowers which graced the wall as if, seeing it for the first time, she found it very beautiful. Then she drew a deep breath and went off in search of Mrs. Larsen.

She hadn't far to go. The lady was lurking between the double doors of the best parlor and the back parlor, which was the one in which the Larsen family usually lived and had their being, provided they were not consuming vast boiled or fish meals in the basement dining room, or drinking coffee at the kitchen table.

"Oh, Mrs. Larsen," said Jill ingratiatingly, and smiled at the large woman towering over her, "I—

Well, it's this way, would you do me a perfectly enormous favor?"

"It all depends," replied Mrs. Larsen darkly. She was a woman impressively massive above the waist. She had long, long feet and surprisingly small hands. She had a white, doughlike face, with currant eyes, and a mass of frizzed, netted and once blond hair on the top of a head set firmly on a thick neck.

"It's Mr. Hardy," explained Jill, in conspiratorial tones. "You remember him? He's been away. He wants to come see me; in fact, he is coming to see me. It's such an awful night," she added pleadingly, "and nowhere to go but the movies . . . So, if we could use your lovely parlor—again?"

Mrs. Larsen inclined her head. She liked Mr. Hardy. She liked him a good deal better than she liked the Bates whippersnapper. Bates, conceded Mrs. Larsen grudgingly, probably had a way with him, but men with a way with them were up to no good and were as a rule far from being good providers. She herself had married a man of considerable charm. Larsen, Able-bodied Seaman. Able-bodied he might have been when he followed his calling but able-bodied he was no longer. Having swallowed the anchor, he had apparently come to the conclusion that active life was concluded for him. He divided his time between the kitchen, with his feet on the stove, in season, engrossed in newspapers and an evil pipe, and the old saloon near South Street at which his cronies of freer but more precarious days turned up to swap tall and salty yarns. A handsome man, he had dowered Mrs. Larsen with six children, of whom one was alive and in parts unknown, and naught besides. Now and then she persuaded him to carry out ashes and garbage or do a bit of carpentry. The one thing she could say for him was that as long as she kept him supplied with tobacco and sufficient funds to quench—in moderation—his thirst, he gave her very little trouble.

She said, grudgingly but with the glimmer of a smile about her tight lips, quivering to a pendulous chin:

"Very well. But no noise, mind. Mrs. Parsons is suffering from her arthritis again. And while it is not decent for a young man and woman to sit together in darkness I would be grateful if you did not burn all the lights. And at twelve sharp Mr. Hardy must be going."

Jill touched her landlady's vast arm. She said gratefully, "You are a dear."

Mrs. Larsen was touched. Few people called her a dear. Few addressed her in any flattering terms whatever. And there was always at the back of her mind that Jill was paid a month in advance. Had she been a month in arrears or just one jump ahead of rent day, it is doubtful if the most dulcet tones and the most poetic form of address would have met with a response.

Jill ran upstairs. Perhaps it wasn't good for the heart but her heart was galloping anyway and the most sedate pace would not have slowed it down. She got out the little blue frock and the matching slip and her last good pair of stockings and the newest slippers. She combed her red shining waves of hair, and did all the necessary and unnecessary things to her face. Dan Hardy—well, she wasn't at all sure she was in love with him but he excited and challenged her. No, you couldn't be in love with a man who disapproved of so many things you liked and who was so very different from any man you'd ever known and thought you were in love with before. But the challenge remained: the desire to turn that disapproval into approval without altering yourself in the least, and the desire to conquer his indifference.

It wasn't indifference, thought Jill; he likes me, he likes me more than he wants to like me. But, she thought, sobering, the lipstick poised, he'll go away and forget me, in no time at all. She wanted terribly, and why she could not have said, to become an important factor in Dan Hardy's life. She thought, pretending scorn of him, These strong silent men! Just like in the movies.

Not that he was very silent. He could talk well, even brilliantly, when he had something to say. But he had no use for manufactured small talk. He had an unexpected and unusual sense of humor but his gaiety was not surface sparkle, as Jimmy's was, nor did he laugh things off as Jimmy did.

She thought, going downstairs again to wait, You're being very silly. Just because he's a little difficult. Jimmy's more your kind, really, you speak the same language.

She honestly did not know, waiting for Dan Hardy's ring at the bell, why the few times she had seen him since their shipboard acquaintance held the power to stimulate and interest her in anticipation and in retrospect. There were times when he exasperated her and she more often disagreed than agreed with him. They had had some extraordinary battles during their short friendship.

The sound she was waiting for came, a sharp pull on the knob, and the bell whined rustily through the house. Mrs. Larsen's one slattern was belowstairs or had gone, clattering her miserable heels, to her top-floor room. Jill, however, sat with her hands folded in her lap and regarded a particularly distasteful study of a red-cheeked little girl offering an apple to a spavined horse. The last time Dan had come to the

23

house she had made the mistake of opening the door to him. Mrs. Larsen had resented that.

Mrs. Larsen wheezed down the hall and opened the door. She said calmly, but with faint surprise, and Jill, listening, chuckled:

"Oh, it's you, Mr. Hardy. Come in. I think Miss Hamilton's in the parlor. Nasty weather we've been having, to be sure."

Dan's deep voice agreed. There was an exchange of inquiries: "You've been well, I hope?" "Fine. And you?" and then Mrs. Larsen appeared at the door of the parlor. "Someone to see you," she informed Jill with a suggestion of archness conflicting astonishingly with her contours.

She lingered a moment to watch Jill sedately shake hands with the tall young man. Then she beamed faintly upon them and departed, leaving the door part way open.

Not until they heard her footsteps die away in the distance did they dare to laugh. Jill said, her eyes crinkled with amusement, "She's an obvious old Gorgon, isn't she? But there's something nice about her. You aren't to stay one minute after midnight and we must have a light burning! But only one. This satisfies her sense of propriety and economy at one and the same time."

Dan Hardy was thirty. He was a big person, big-boned, long-muscled, and there was not quite enough flesh on his frame. He was very dark and, Jill fancied, almost always tanned. He was, she thought further, the most perfectly co-ordinated person she had ever seen. He did not waste energy in gesture. When he moved it was, she told herself, all of one piece. He had very brilliant eyes and heavy brows and an abrupt, forceful nose, bumpy across the bridge where it had been broken in football. In fact, she decided, looking at him smiling, his face was entirely crooked, one eyebrow higher than the other, and the effect of his sudden grin slightly lopsided. His teeth were his best feature, startlingly white against his dark skin.

"Well," he inquired, "what's the matter? Or don't you like my face?"

"Very much," Jill told him, "only it's a bit out of drawing." She cocked her impertinent red head on one side and regarded him coolly. "You look," she said, "a little like an Indian who's been left out in the rain."

He shrugged his big shoulders. "They tell me that my great-great-grandfather—"

"Pocahontas?" asked Jill, wide-eyed.

He laughed. "Well, it's a family legend anyway," he said. "Look here, must we stand around until midnight? Or may I have a chair?"

He selected a large round one plentifully plushed

25

and sat down in it, leaning his head back against the lace tidy which spanned the back. Jill took the corner of a horsehair sofa and sat bolt upright in order to keep from sliding off. There was a brass ash tray on the fireplace mantel, a souvenir of Atlantic City, and Dan made a long reach and set it on the arm of his chair. He offered his pack of cigarettes to Jill and she took one.

Presently they sat smoking in a companionable silence and then she asked:

"Any luck?"

"None." He grinned and then sobered. He had been, she knew, to Detroit on the trail of a job. "Or, rather, lots, all bad. I was a day too late. But I heard of a berth here in town. It's desk work," he said, frowning, "but it will have to serve until I can get something else. I wish," he added, "that I'd had sense enough to stay in Central America. If I'd hung around there would always be things I could find to do, enough to keep me in food and tobacco and then when a big job got under way I'd be on hand." He moved his shoulders again impatiently. "But I'd saved a little money, and when you've been away from New York for any length of time you get to thinking that you're missing an opportunity if you don't get back."

Jill said lightly, "If you hadn't come back—and on that special boat—we wouldn't have met."

She wanted to hear him say, "Of course—and it was worth it, all the disappointment that followed after we landed."

But he didn't say it. He merely said, "That's so," and looked at her thoughtfully.

She said, conscious of disappointment and angry at herself:

"If you get the desk job?"

"I'll get it," he said calmly, stretching his long legs, "I've all the qualifications. There'll be a lot of drudgery and battling over blueprints and there won't be much pay. But I'll be at the office tomorrow before nine and I'll have the job."

She told herself, I should dislike him, really; he's so—so darned cocksure. But she realized that he was cocksure not because of any bravado, but because he had certainty. He knew himself and his job. She stubbed out the cigarette, refused another, and leaned back cautiously against the inhospitable horsehair. Dan said, smiling:

"Tell me about yourself."

"There isn't anything to tell. I've answered a lot of ads. They didn't come to anything. Oh, yes, I tried out on an amateur hour . . . I should have known better," she said a little bitterly.

Dan said gently:

"It's been in the back of your mind all along, hasn't it, that one day you'd make good on the radio?"

Jill looked at him in genuine astonishment.

"Lord, no," she said, and laughed. "I gave that up ages ago. The first audition finished me. You see, I have a rather nice voice but the mike does things to it. It just doesn't go over. I hadn't any high hopes, only you get paid for even a flop on an amateur hour and I thought it might be fun. Then there was a faint chance that all those grave gentlemen who listened to me the first time had been wrong. Well, they weren't."

He persisted:

"But perhaps it's something that can be overcome in the control room? Or that lessons would help?"

Jill shook her head. "And what would I use for money even if lessons would help?"

"It was just a suggestion," he told her. "I was thinking, even if it never came to anything, it would be good for you to have something to work toward— some definite goal."

"Meantime I have to eat," she reminded him. She looked at him with something very like hostility, comparing him with Jimmy, who could let tomorrow take care of itself. Even his clothes . . . Jimmy's clothes were expensive, well cut and distinguished even when shabby. They were usually shabby. He bought himself the costliest best when in funds, and even when

28

they were worn they had a certain air. Dan, however, wore serviceable tweeds; ready-made, they did not fit him within a mile of perfection; they were just clothes, and that was all.

He said mildly, "You could eat. But if you had some purpose—beyond eating?"

Jill jumped up and went to the mantel and leaned against it looking down at the unilluminated gas log. She said, "Dan, you make me so *darned* mad. Does everyone have to have a Purpose? You talk like someone lecturing to women's clubs. If wanting a roof over my head and three meals a day isn't a sufficient purpose, well, I'll have to do without one!"

Dan came to his feet and smiled at her lazily. He said, "Sorry I made you sore. Look—" he walked over to the tall narrow windows, drew aside the shabby velvet draperies and the net glass curtains and looked out—"it's stopped raining. Go upstairs and put on something sensible and we'll go for a walk."

"I don't want to go for a walk."

"Yes, you do," he said infuriatingly, "do you good. Get your blood in circulation. Besides, I don't want to sit here till twelve o'clock and quarrel with you. We won't outdoors. It must be the room," he said, regarding it appraisingly.

"You're under no compulsion to sit at all—" began Jill furiously, and then laughed. "Dan Hardy, you're

29

the most maddening man I ever met. Okay . . . I'll be back in five minutes."

"Three," said Dan.

She flew upstairs and collided with Mrs. Larsen on the second landing. Mrs. Larsen steadied her with a large arm. She said, "What's the matter?" and her currant eyes gleamed dully. If they'd had a quarrel it hadn't been a loud one.

Jill said, gasping, "It's stopped raining. We're going for a walk," and escaped. Mrs. Larsen stood looking after her and shook her head. Things were different in her day. Gaslight turned to a blue flicker and Larsen's salty advances. But she was too smart for him. She'd married him out of hand. Now and then it occurred to her to wonder if he hadn't been too smart for her.

Jill ripped off the blue frock which, she thought hotly, Dan hadn't even noticed and changed back to the tweed and pull-over, the worn shoes and the felt hat. She had a good warm coat, probably too warm, but there was nothing else except the raincoat, unless she wore the three-quarter coat with the fur collar which belonged to her one good suit. She wore it and, thus arrayed, went on downstairs again, thinking, I hope someday I'll live on a ground floor.

The night, when she and Dan emerged from the house, was clear with stars shining, though the pavements were still wet. There was a spring wind and a sense of newness and freshness in the air. Jill put her hand on Dan's arm and they walked briskly. She took the biggest strides she could in order to keep up with him, but a few blocks of that pace gave her a stitch in her side. She said ruefully:

"You'll have to shorten your steps, Dan; I can't lengthen mine any more!"

"I'm sorry," he told her and accommodated his stride to hers. He drew a deep breath and pushed his battered hat back on his head. He said, "I never got the house habit, somehow. This is more like it."

She said rebelliously:

"I don't know why the dickens I'm doing this. After all, it's no treat to me, I tramp the streets half the day looking for work."

"Poor kid," said Dan, and put his big hand over hers.

She was an honest little person. She said quickly, "Oh, don't be sorry for me, Dan; I'm not sorry for myself, really, I suppose I was just looking for a touch of sympathy. You know, weak woman, strong man." She laughed, but he did not laugh with her. He said gravely:

"I *am* sorry for you, Jill. You—you'll hate this, but I have to say it again—you're so purposeless, you let yourself drift with every wind. I can't see that. If I didn't know where I was headed and why I was headed there, there'd be no sense to anything."

Jill said slowly, "Perhaps you're right. When I'm with you I think so. Then other times . . . Well, I get to thinking what tomorrow will bring. And it hasn't been my fault," she said strongly, "I thought I was safe. I had a home. I was content. I had the average education of the girl in the small town who has no great talent, who doesn't want to teach or nurse. I thought I'd go on like that, having friends and a good time in our own way, keeping house for my father until I married. But suddenly there wasn't any home and there wasn't anyone to whom I could turn. I hadn't been trained for anything and I had to get out and do the best I could. I'm not apologizing for myself, Dan, it's just that we look at things so differently."

"I suppose so," he admitted. "You see, ever since I was a kid building bridges with stones over a brook on a Pennsylvania farm I knew I was going to be an engineer. My people hadn't much. But they managed, and I managed and I supplemented what money they could spare with hard work and by winning scholarships. I couldn't let it all go, I couldn't turn traitor to the sacrifices they'd made for me, or to myself." She felt rather than saw how dogged the set of his jaw was when he said that. "And I can't give it up now, not for easier jobs and more money. I suppose you know that there are easier jobs and more money even today? And if you're willing to play ball . . . I was offered the supervising of a building job just before I went down on that Central American business. It had quite a title: Field Engineer. And there was a lot of money in it. Not in salary, but in graft. My employers had to shell out plenty to venial inspectors and the like, but there were others who were willing to trade with me and make it worth my while. All I had to do was pass certain material and certain labor and accept certain bids. I suppose a lot of people would think I was a fool to turn it down. They'd argue someone was going to get it, why not Dan Hardy? Shoddy material, cheap, dishonest contractors . . . it all meant more than the comfort of the people who'd live in that apartment house someday. It meant, perhaps, their lives."

Jill cried, "Of course, you couldn't do anything else. I wouldn't for the world have you take on anything like that." She added hastily, lest he think her becoming possessive, "No one would, in their senses. But a decent, honorable desk job somewhere . . . Gosh, Dan, not many people build bridges and railroads."

"Perhaps not. When they do I want to be there." He added, "Have you ever been in a construction camp?"

33

"Heavens! No!"

"Naturally. You'd hate it probably," he said, and for a moment her heart slowed and then began to beat furiously. Did he mean . . . ? Could he . . . ? But of course not. He hadn't said anything, ever, hadn't made the least gesture, not even on board ship those glowing, romantic, moonlit nights. But he liked her. If he didn't like her, why did he come to see her, why did he keep in touch? Or was it because he was lonely?

She said, and laughed:

"Probably I would. Look here, I've never asked you this. Isn't there a girl somewhere waiting for a bridge to be built or a track laid?"

"No," he answered, "there isn't. Oh, I've had—ideas. You get very lonely sometimes."

So that *is* it, thought Jill and told herself that she didn't care, he didn't mean anything to her anyway, really.

But he went on, "I suppose I never found one who'd see that there was adventure in hardship. Women don't understand about building . . . building something substantial, concrete, enduring, building your life that way, your lives together. It's funny, you'd think they would understand; after all, they are the real builders . . . or their grandmothers were. I don't know much about this generation."

He looked down on her. She was walking more

slowly, dragging a little at his arm. He exclaimed, "You're tired! I'm certainly anything you want to call me for making you walk half over New York."

She said, "I'm tired, all right, and a little cold." She shivered. The good suit coat wasn't warm and the wind wasn't warm either.

Dan said contritely, "Let's find a place and get some coffee. There must be an all-night place around here. If it comes to that, it isn't very late."

They found a place, cheerful, clean, white-tiled, and sat at a counter and drank coffee and ate doughnuts. Dan said enthusiastically, "I've a theory about dunking. It as an art." He demonstrated, to Jill's vast amusement. She was, she found, hungry, and the color was high in her cheeks and her red hair curled under the brim of the disreputable hat. She looked very attractive and she knew it from the admiring regard of the counterman who brought her extra cream and called her "Sister."

Dan knew it too. He said it, oblivious of the taxi drivers and odd fry all about them, oblivious to the envious counterman and the short-order cook peering in at the doorway, an apron about his vast middle and a huge cap on one side of his bald head.

"I think," remarked Dan gravely, "that you are the prettiest girl I ever saw."

That was like him. Out with it, no frills. Jimmy said

things differently. He also said them more easily. This remark coming from Dan was in the nature of a triumph.

Jill said, "That's nice of you, Dan. Haven't been around much, have you?"

He said, "I've been around a lot." He looked at her, coffee cup heavy in one hand, doughnut not any too light in the other, "But you could do with a little more weight," he said critically.

Jill dissolved into wild and helpless laughter. She gasped, "You're impossible. First you hand a girl a flower and then you hit her with a brick. Give me another doughnut. Perhaps I'm undernourished after all."

It was past midnight when he left her at the Larsen door. "Got your key?" he inquired.

"Yes. Here it is." She watched him fit it into the lock. "I'm sleepy," she said, and yawned frankly.

"You need exercise," he told her.

"Will you stop talking to me like a mother?" She added, "If you knew how I had to work on the Larsen to get that key. She didn't think I rated it. No one under fifty had a key. But I conquered. She thinks that possibly I am to be trusted."

She knew, however, that Mrs. Larsen rarely slept. When Jill let herself in nights, no matter how softly, she would pop out unexpectedly and wrapped in an appalling gray-flannel garment ostensibly to wish her lodger good night. But Jill knew better. Mrs. Larsen had to be very sure that her young lady paying guest was coming home alone.

The door swung open. Jill held out her hand and Dan took it. She said, feeling his warm, hard clasp, "Good night, Dan, and thanks for everything . . . especially the doughnuts."

"Good night," he said. "I'll call you, in a day or so."

He was gone, whistling, down the steps. Jill stared after him. Then she shut the door and started slowly upstairs. Her feet hurt, she had had one doughnut too many, her holiday mood was over, she was tired in every muscle and dead for sleep. What an evening!

Still if, like Jimmy, Dan had told her "don't be so unkind"?

But he hadn't. She told herself, toiling upward, aware that from the second floor back a door had opened and that presently, like a great gray owl, Mrs. Larsen would appear, I don't know why I bother with him. He isn't fun, like Jimmy. I'm certainly not in love with him.

She wasn't in love with either of them, of course not. She wasn't in love with anyone. She was free, white, and over twenty-one, and out of a job. She was so sleepy she could hardly respond to Mrs. Larsen's routine greeting, and tomorrow was another day.

But, she thought triumphantly, just dropping off to dreams a little later, he had told her that she was the prettiest girl he'd ever seen.

CHAPTER III

In the morning the sun shone bravely and Jill awakened to see the flickering pattern on faded shade and uneven floor. She stretched lazily, luxuriously, feeling the pull of her lithe young muscles, and then crossed her arms behind her head yawning. Breakfast waited on the window sill: a pint of milk, and in a paper box a buttered round of coffee cake and an orange. Very proper, she reflected, smiling to herself, vitamins and minerals, starch and sweet . . . proteins . . . did bread contain proteins? She had forgotten. Not that it mattered.

Mrs. Larsen closed her eyes to the window-sill cache. Cooking in the rooms was forbidden, except in the case of the second floor parlor and bedroom; but, being a just woman, she had no objection to a bottle of milk. Jill reflected that if she didn't get a job pretty soon it would grow too warm, as summer followed spring, for her window-sill pantry. But she wasn't worried, particularly. Something would turn up, it always had.

39

She rose, pulled a warm robe about her, thrust her feet into heelless slippers, and clattered out of bed and down the hall to the bathroom she shared with the two other inmates of the next to the top floor: the elderly typist who had been looking for a job for half a year and the "retired" seamstress. Jill liked them both although she sometimes grumbled when Miss Fawkes, the typist, forgot to wash the ring off the tub, or Miss Allen, the seamstress, took all the available hot water. Miss Fawkes had taught her to type—not professionally, but with two fingers, though accurately enough, and Miss Allen was sweet about sewing on shoulder straps for her, altering a hem, or turning a cuff.

Mrs. Larsen's lodging house was for ladies only. Jill reflected now and then that it might be a little more exciting if a man or so were permitted to house under that roof, but Mrs. Larsen had no use for any form of coeducation. Once when Jimmy was looking for a place to live, shortly after Jill had found the Larsen retreat, she had pleaded for him: "It would just be temporary, Mrs. Larsen, and he could pay two weeks in advance." But Mrs. Larsen, although the mere mention of the word "advance" caused her to prick up her large white ears, was adamant. There was always trouble, she said darkly, when you mixed the sexes. And added—not too cryptically—that she couldn't be everywhere at once!

40

This morning's bath water was on the tepid side. Either Miss Allen or Miss Fawkes had risen early or else, thought Jill, shivering under a sponge bath, standing on one leg like a heron on the thin bath mat, Larsen had forgotten to shake up the fire. It was, however, all in the day's chances and she was philosophical about it. She had lived in worse places and suffered more inconveniences. She could always think about them and believe that Mrs. Larsen's was a palace by comparison. She recalled with no felicity the hot place under the roof in which she had stayed during her Coney Island experience. Noisy, disreputable, odorous . . . children crying and women quarreling and strange, strawheaded blondes, with lined and weary faces, leaning from dirty neighboring windows.

Now and then when a job paid well Jill had some of the luxuries. Once she had lived in a modest, well-run, attractive hotel for women; and in Mrs. Emory's house she had come downstairs to breakfast and been served by a young and friendly butler, in a large and sunny dining room. She hated to think of Mrs. Emory's when she was hungry . . . Olga made such marvelous popovers and coffee! And during her seasonal stay in Palm Beach, selling smart frocks at a smarter shop, she had shared a tiny, charming apartment over the store with two other girls. Sunshine and blue water, pretty girls on bicycles, handsome

41

women in wheel chairs, delectable breakfasts, and generally an idle man or two who'd buy lunch or dinner.

"From riches to rags," she murmured to herself and galloped back to her bedroom to dress.

She put on the second best, the job-hunting suit, hunter green for luck; it had an air of prosperity. The blouse was soft white silk, and with polishing the shoes would have to do. She squeezed the orange into a glass and drank it, pulp and all, drank the milk and ate the bun before powdering her nose and applying her lipstick. Then the jacket with the notched collar and the matching green hat. The run in her left stocking didn't show, she had caught it before it went too far.

A last look around, a perkier tilt to the hat, and she was off to buy the morning paper and to stand on the corner exchanging wisecracks with Tony the newsstand boy, the paper folded to the want-ad columns.

At noon, after three fruitless interviews, she went into a drugstore and had a cup of coffee and a sandwich. There was gooey chocolate cake, probably not very good, under a spotty glass cover. Jill looked at it longingly. She had a healthy appetite. But she wanted a pack of cigarettes, and she couldn't break into the hat money and her savings would not last forever. A roof came first and then food . . . chocolate cake wasn't food exactly, it was frivolity.

She walked to the Madison Avenue shop where she had seen the hat. She bought it, and carried it home in its round little box. It would be divine, she thought, with the best suit, the one she wore when she had a job and was therefore, she considered, entitled to wear it. Mrs. Larsen emerging, as she entered, from the rear quarters looked at her with disapproval.

"Find something?"

"Not yet, but I've a promise—"

That wasn't so. But she could see Mrs. Larsen counting the days and weeks under that peculiar mass of hair. So Jill smiled and tilted her chin, and spoke bravely of a nonexistent promise.

"Been buying a hat?" persisted her landlady.

Jill suppressed a wild impulse to reply gravely, "No, indeed. This is the Empire State Building, isn't it wonderful how nicely they package it?" She answered, however, "Yes . . . I needed one badly . . . and it was *such* a bargain."

She rested the box on the stair rail and began to undo the string. Sooner or later Mrs. Larsen would see the hat, either on Jill's head or in Jill's bedroom. She might as well exhibit it now and be done with it.

"It's plain," commented Mrs. Larsen, whose taste ran to feathers, drooping, and flowers, upstanding. Jill nodded. She turned the hat on her head and said fondly, "But—it has an air."

43

Mrs. Larsen said dubiously, "I suppose so," and then turned away. Jill had the hat back in the box and her foot on the next step when the older woman recollected something. She said, "Oh, I forgot. A Mrs. Amory phoned, wants you to call her."

"Amory? Oh, Emory," corrected Jill and her heart beat faster and the color crept up to her high cheekbones. "Golly!"

She set the box on the stairs and went to the back hall in which Mrs. Larsen had thoughtfully installed a pay booth for her guests. Incoming calls they might receive on her own telephone, but outgoing calls were paid for on the nail.

Jill fished in her pocketbook for a nickel, lifted the instrument, dialed.

Mrs. Larsen, following, lingered, her head on one side.

She didn't hear much.

"Frederick? This is Miss Hamilton. Is Mrs. Emory at home?"

A pause.

"Oh, Mrs. Emory . . . Jill Hamilton . . . did you call me? Yes. No, I haven't. But how dear of you! Of course I'll go. I'm so glad I came in just now. Three o'clock . . . Yes . . . Yes . . ." She repeated a Park Avenue address and a name. She said, "Thank you so very much. Yes, of course, I'll let you know at once. Good-bye."

Up banged the receiver. Jill whirled about, caught Mrs. Larsen about her large and solid waist and did a most fantastic tango. "Here, here," said that lady, laughing in spite of herself, "what's happened, come into money?"

"A job's happened," cried Jill, "at least I think it's a job."

"What kind of a job?"

Jill stopped. She released her cumbersome partner. She said, in mild surprise, pushing her hat from her brow, "Why, I don't know exactly," and fled upstairs while Mrs. Larsen, still panting slightly from her recent involuntary exertions, gazed after her with an expression of mingled bewilderment and doubt.

Jill, washing her face and hands, brushing her hair, brushing, too, the very best suit on the off chance, hunting out the good gloves and bag and the one possible pair of shoes, whistled to herself. Mrs. Emory had said, "You will like Mr. Dennis very much . . . and I am sure he will like you." Then there had been something about grandchildren.

Jill sat down on her bed, her hand and arm thrust into one of the pair of stockings she had been saving against an emergency. No, no runs, praises be! Grandchildren? It wasn't possible that Mrs. Emory thought

45

she could become a nursemaid or nursery governess. She hadn't really paid much attention to anything except the name and the address of the prospective employer. Well, nursery maid or nursery governess, it didn't matter. She'd take it on and brush up on her A B C's.

At three o'clock, to the minute, Jill presented herself at the door of Mr. Charles Dennis. Mr. Dennis lived, it appeared, in one of the last houses left intact on Park Avenue. Narrow gray stone, high, with window boxes of ivy, it sat firmly between two apartment houses, defying the passage of time, chance, and change.

Jill squared her shoulders, conscious that the best suit though past its prime was still chic and became her very well . . . soft brown wool, with a trim little skirt, and the three-quarter coat collared in beaver that she had worn last night with Dan. The new hat was just right and the brown pumps looked almost new. The gloves were *almost* new. And the bag looked so prosperous that no one would guess its emptiness.

An elderly, amiable manservant opened the door to her and, when she spoke her name, smiled. He announced, somewhat to her astonishment, that Mr. Arden would see her, in the library.

The foyer was square, simply and beautifully furnished, and on her way to the library Jill caught a glimpse of a long drawing room, a smaller drawing room with what she judged was the dining room back of it. The library itself had great windows opening on a large back yard and smelled pleasantly of leather bindings. Books climbed to the ceiling on every side, except for the spaces occupied by the windows and a fireplace.

A young man rose from behind the flat-topped desk as Jill entered. He dismissed the servant briefly, smiled bleakly at Jill, and indicated a chair. Then he said briskly:

"I am Mr. Dennis's secretary, Miss Hamilton. He has asked me to see you and discuss your qualifications."

Mr. Arden was at first glance a nondescript young man, mousy in coloring, with a high forehead and large tortoise-shell-rimmed spectacles. He looked scholarly, thirty-five, courteous and timid. Now he removed the glasses and laid them on the desk and Jill became aware that his mouth was thin and secretive, his eyes almost repellently intelligent, and his chin forceful. She also perceived that he was probably ten years younger than she had thought him.

He leaned back in the big chair and fitted his fingertips very precisely together.

"Mrs. Emory," he said, in a tone of infuriating patronage, "has spoken very highly of you." He shrugged, smiled and looked skeptical. "I have been interviewing," he went on, "various young ladies, for several weeks and have almost despaired of finding anyone whom I could conscientiously recommend to Mr. Dennis. You see, this has been a process of elimination. The verdict is not up to me. I merely, shall we say, weed."

"If you insist," responded Jill docilely.

"If I insist?" he demanded and regarded her with almost human interest.

She said meekly, "If you insist on saying 'weed.' I don't."

Mr. Arden bent his brows. Then his face cleared and he laughed. ".I see," he murmured, " a sense of humor. Well, that is decidedly in your favor." He leaned forward and looked at her directly. "You weren't told just what the position would be?"

"No," said Jill, "I wasn't." She grinned at him suddenly. "And you are making it very mysterious. What is it, espionage on Park Avenue or nonprofessional attendant to the village idiot?"

"My dear young woman!" exclaimed Mr. Arden, thoroughly shocked.

"No?" said Jill and settled back in her chair. "Disappointing, I calls it," she murmured.

Mr. Arden said severely:

"Humor is all very well in its place. Levity—is

48

another matter. I assume you know who Mr. Dennis is?"

"No," admitted Jill, "I don't. But if he's a friend of Mrs. Emory's, that's good enough for me."

Mr. Arden looked pained. He was not offering recommendations, that was Jill's function. At the same time he was thinking fast. He was thinking, Young enough, not too young, pretty, wears her clothes well, speaks as a lady speaks—the voice, at any rate—looks as if she had a will of her own, which is all right up to a certain point.

He explained dryly:

"Mr. Dennis is a man of considerable attainment in his field—which is that of the essay. In recent years he has retired from active business and devoted himself to his writing, as an avocation. He has living with him his two granddaughters: Mary, who is fourteen, and Sally, who is seventeen. They attend day school in New York as Mr. Dennis does not wish to be separated from them. They are the daughters of his only son, Edgar, who, together with his wife, the children's mother, was killed in an airplane accident three years ago. Mr. Dennis has latterly been seeking for a suitable companion for his grandchildren. They have of course passed the nurse and even the governess stage. He wants someone who will make her home with them, be with them before and after school hours and during vacations, and who will devote herself to their interests. Various older women have been suggested, and last year one was engaged to fill the post. "But," he added delicately, "the two girls have been rather— indulged, and Mrs. Peters found them difficult to handle. When you see Mr. Dennis you will realize how this came about. It was Mrs. Emory, a lifelong friend, who suggested that the companion be younger, not too young, of course, but young enough to appreciate the girls' point of view. Now may I ask you a few questions?"

He asked them. Where she was born, how old she was, what her education had been and her background. And then:

"Just what can you do?"

"Frankly," replied Jill and smiled at him, "I can do a little of everything. I'm not a specialist." She added, "Suppose you ask me what I can't do."

He said, frowning slightly, "Do you play contract?"

Astonished, Jill said, "Yes, and rather well if I do say it myself. I've been a cruise hostess, you know, and contract was indicated. Also I played rather frequently when I was with Mrs. Emory." She added wickedly, "I am also lucky at poker."

"I doubt," said Mr. Arden austerely, "if poker will be required." But his intelligent eyes had a gleam which Jill diagnosed as humor. She became at once a little more inclined toward him. He wasn't perhaps quite the prig and pedant she had thought him.

"Do you swim?"

"Yes, very well," she said calmly.

"Tennis?"

"Indifferent."

"Golf?"

"Not often," Jill said, "but I can learn. I played a little at Palm Beach a few seasons ago."

The pale eyebrows lifted. "Good. You are fond of reading?"

"Very," said Jill, "if I like the book!"

"Are you at all musical?"

"I sing," said Jill, astonished.

"Splendid," said Mr. Arden heartily. "Sally has a rather charming little voice, unfortunately she needs—encouragement. Do you play?"

"Enough to accompany myself," Jill told him.

He said rapidly, "You must excuse the inquisition. You see, your position in a way will be that of hostess —for the girls, that is. I assume you are an extrovert?"

"Good heavens," cried Jill, "am I?" She looked as grieved as a child, and Mr. Arden said hastily:

"That is to say, you are fond of people, you enjoy them?"

But Jill was laughing. She said cheerfully, "I think

51

you mean, am I a good mixer? Well, Mr. Arden, in the last seven years I've had to be!"

He said doubtfully, "That is also very good; but I must ask you this: have you any—ties?"

Jill thought furiously, A neat way of inquiring about my morals, I must say. She smiled, however, with her lips and answered smoothly:

"No, Mr. Arden, I have not. I have men friends, of course, as any normal girl would have. I shall expect to see them on the proper occasions. They are, I assure you, entirely suitable young men. But I am not engaged to be married," she concluded, "if that is what you mean. And I assume it was what you meant?"

Mr. Arden had become a deep, unbecoming red. He said, hastily, "Of course. You understand that if you are employed by Mr. Dennis you will be able to see your friends; this will be, to all intents and purposes, your home." He looked at the moment very disapproving. "Mr. Dennis insists on that," he added.

There were a few more questions. Her religion, her adaptability, her power of judgment and discernment, and Jill said flatly:

"Really, Mr. Arden, that is something one can't theorize about. I think I am a fair judge of people, and moderately just. But you'd have to see me in action, wouldn't you?"

"Quite," agreed Mr. Arden, and rose. Jill rose also.

He said quickly, "Now, if you please, will you wait here a moment?"

The library door opened and a girl came in. She was about Jill's age, blond, overthin, with a petulant prettiness. She said, "Hello, Chester," carelessly and Mr. Arden winced, then she added, "Oh, sorry. I was looking for Uncle Charles."

She glanced at Jill and away again. So Mr. Dennis had a niece as well as granddaughters. How did she fit into the picture? Jill wondered.

Arden murmured something and the two disappeared. Jill sat waiting, her ankles crossed, and her fingers crossed as well. She didn't especially like Mr. Dennis's secretary, but he seemed to know his job. She didn't know much about hers, as yet, provided she got it. But she assumed that she was to be playmate and duenna for a couple of spoiled youngsters. She would make a fourth at bridge and a partner at tennis and an accompanist. Probably she would oversee their invitations and their boy friends. Well, she'd try almost anything once, she reflected, and she did so like this house with its atmosphere of substantial good living.

The door opened again and Arden re-entered, preceded by a tall, very lean man. Jill took one look at him and fell irrevocably in love.

Charles Dennis was in his seventies. He was six feet two. He had an aquiline face and the finest blue eyes

53

Jill had ever seen. He had a charming smile. He looked a little like the pictures of William Gillette, which were interchangeable in Jill's mind with Sherlock Holmes, the idol of her girlhood.

Mr. Dennis had a deep, resonant voice and a firm, warm handclasp. Arden had vanished silently and mysteriously and Dennis said:

"Come here and let me look at you."

Jill did so obediently. She smiled up at the old man and he smiled down at her. He said gently:

"My efficient secretary brings me good report of you. And my old friend Carolyn Emory even better. That isn't the point. The point is, will you be happy with us, my dear?"

She wanted to say, I'd be happy near you anywhere. She felt the unaccustomed tears in her throat. She thought, If those girls are brats and don't adore him, I'll murder them! He reminded her, very faintly, of her own father, as he might have been had he lived. He reminded her of home and lamplight and wisdom and peace and of the love of God and of one's fellow man. He was as real as poverty and as enduring as oak.

She said, "Mr. Dennis, if you'd give me a chance—"

Charles Dennis lowered himself into the desk chair and said, "Come over here, Jill."

She went and stood beside him. He said, smiling:

"Carolyn has told me a good deal about you. You've

tried your capable little hand at any number of things, haven't you?"

"Yes," she said. Her chin went up. "But at nothing," she told him, "of which I need be ashamed."

"I'm sure of that," he said, "and you needn't be on the defensive with me, my child." He looked at her a moment. "I wish my two had something of your gumption!" he added. Then he asked, "You haven't been working for a long time, have you?"

"Not for several months." She wanted to say, But that isn't why I want the job, altogether. I want it because I think you're such a grand person. Because I'd like to make good . . . for you.

Dennis had opened a drawer and taken out a flat thin checkbook. Now he was writing in it. He looked up to say, "Does two hundred a month meet with your approval?"

Jill gasped. "Two hundred," she began, but Mr. Dennis wasn't listening.

"Let me see," he told her, "this is the fifteenth of April. Suppose we say the first of May. That will give you time to buy what you need. I am assuming that you will need things . . . most girls do. We leave for Long Island the first of June." He blotted the check, tore it out of the book, slipped it in an envelope and handed it to her. He said, "I realize that you will have to have certain fripperies . . . my two girls are very

55

gregarious, they go places and do things." He smiled and his blue eyes twinkled. "This will take care of your expenses," he told her. "I consider them business expenses of course, and perfectly legitimate."

Jill took the envelope. She did not open it. Had she done so and perceived the fact that Charles Dennis had given her five hundred dollars to spend on "fripperies" she would have dropped dead at his feet. She was flushed, murmuring her gratitude.

As she walked with him toward the library door it opened and Arden and the blond girl came in. Arden said quickly, "I'm sorry. I had forgotten to ask Miss Hamilton if she rides."

Jill said, breathless, "Yes, of course. I mean, I did at home, and while I haven't ridden a great deal since coming to New York . . ."

"I am sure," interrupted Mr. Dennis, "that Miss Hamilton will satisfy even your difficult standards, Chester." He smiled at Jill and said, "Have you met the other member of my household? My niece, Miss Henshaw. . . . Elise, this is Jill Hamilton, who is coming to us in a week or so."

Elise held out a long slim hand and Jill took it. The other girl said languidly, "How nice . . ." and Jill knew at once that so far as Elise was concerned it wasn't nice at all.

Ten minutes later she was out in the street and on

her way to Mrs. Emory's. She had to talk to someone. She thought, clutching the envelope and suppressing her desire to open it, I've got a job! And was aware that in obtaining that job she had made one friend and at least one enemy.

CHAPTER IV

PROVIDENTIALLY Mrs. Emory was at home. If she hadn't been, Jill would have exploded, disintegrated, blown up, burst, vanished into thin air. She debated on the way to the bus which would take her up Riverside Drive, "What shall I do if she isn't in? I haven't a child's idea where Jimmy is and I haven't heard from Dan. If only Helen were in town. If I don't talk to someone . . . if someone doesn't pinch me . . ."

Helen Elliott was Jill's closest woman friend, a sprightly brunette of Jill's age. They had held three brief jobs together. Jill had met Helen when they were both clerking in a department-store bookshop during the Christmas rush. Helen's positions, prior and subsequent, had been as colorful and as varied as Jill's. All winter Helen had been, of all things, a hostess in a tourist camp in Florida. It was a tourist camp de luxe, with parking space, tents, cabins, two hotels, one moderately priced and one more expensive, every kind of amusement, and a great recreation hall over which Helen had presided all season. But the season would soon close and Helen would once more be on the branch.

In the bus Jill could no longer contain herself. She took Mr. Dennis's chaste white envelope from her handbag, opened it, pulled at the corner of the yellow slip there enclosed, slipped it out just far enough to read the figures and gasping, exclaimed, "Holy Moses!" in a loud and frightened voice, to the amusement, astonishment, and consternation of her fellow passengers, each reaction dependent upon age and sex.

The salary, thought Jill, was, to be honest, absurd. The check was absolutely ridiculous. She returned it to the envelope with trembling hands, tucked the envelope in the zippered portion of her handbag and leaned back against the seat. She closed her eyes and saw white linen suits, buckskin shoes, smart little hats, dark, dashing blouses; she saw lawns and chiffons and dimities, cotton evening frocks, lace frocks, lingerie, bathing suits, play suits. It was characteristic of her that she did not see a savings account. She did harbor a fleeting notion that it might be well to lay something aside for a less sunny day but, on the other hand, Mr. Dennis expected her to expend his check on the sartorial façade which was, he had assured her, a legitimate business item. It would therefore be like a doctoring of one's swindle sheet, expense account, to provide future safety out of present prodigality!

She had such sugar-plum visions behind her closed lids that of course she passed her street, came to herself with a start, rang the bell with fury and alighted, followed by sundry speculative glances.

Mrs. Emory lived in a severe and narrow house in the Seventies, off the Drive. Inside it was cheerful in the extreme, brimming over with canaries, parrots, fat and docile cats, beaming servants, Waterford glass, Sheraton pieces, modern chintz, and photographs of most of the people Mrs. Emory had known and loved during her seventy-six years of life.

She would see Jill, thank fortune. Jill was received first by Frederick, the rotund butler, and then by Miss Reynolds, the splinterlike companion for whom Jill had once substituted. Miss Reynolds exhibited a rare smile, like curdled milk, offered Jill a bony hand, cold as a landlord's heart, squeaked at her in a voice which needed oiling and was no compliment to her native Sussex, and ushered her upstairs to Mrs. Emory's sitting room.

This was a cheerful apartment, at the back of the house overlooking a sizable yard which boasted, in season, grass and ramblers and a bird bath. The room was large, clean, and untidy. It contained three canaries, two cats, the senior parrot who squawked, "Hello, what's the big idea of coming so late?" as Jill entered. The walls were hidden by photographs. The chairs

60

were deep, there was a sewing table, at least fifty magazines, a radio, bookshelves, footstools, and a collection
of Copenhagen porcelain.

Mrs. Emory sat in a large chair and knitted reluctantly. She frowned and counted aloud. She looked up
as Miss Reynolds squeaked at her and said, "Oh, come
in, Jill, my dear. Wait a minute. Sit down here. That
will be all for now, Reynolds."

Swishing a taffeta petticoat, recently returned to
fashion but worn—or one like it—since girlhood,
Reynolds departed.

"Purl two," groaned Mrs. Emory. She flung down
the knitting, sighed, took off horn-rimmed spectacles
and looked at Jill. "I loathe knitting," she said fiercely,
"I do it only because it is expected of me. Years behind
me, time on my hands. Nonsense."

She took a cigarette from a lacquer box, and mo-
tioned to Jill. "Have one," she said. She lit hers and
leaned back. She was a very small woman, quite
plump, with white hair which she kept faintly blue.
She had snapping black eyes and beautiful, entirely
synthetic teeth. She demanded, "Well, what happened?"

Jill had cast her hat and coat aside. She had treated
them with utmost disrespect. It didn't matter now.
She could afford to ignore their past importance. She

replied, "I got the job. Oh, Mrs. Emory, Mr. Dennis is the most marvelous person . . . I'm crazy about him."

"Charles Dennis," commented Mrs. Emory reflectively, "has had sex appeal since he was six years old. He'll have it when he's eighty."

Jill said, "Look . . . I don't understand. He offered me two hundred a month and," she dropped her voice, and whispered, as if the photographs on the walls had sentient ears, "he gave me five hundred to buy clothes and things. I don't understand at all." She then inquired in a small and startled voice, "Is—is he a little mad?"

"Yes," answered Mrs. Emory comfortably, "he is. He's always been mad in a perfectly nice way. Not mad enough, however. I've known him all his life, practically. He's a year or so younger than I am. At one time we were engaged to be married. But I had romantic notions . . . I had known Charles so long and so well and our families were so smug about it, as if they had arranged it from our cradles. Anyway I eloped with Mr. Emory. There was quite a scandal at the time," she went on complacently, "as Mr. Emory was many years my senior and had been married before. At all events we lived in Europe for a number of years. When we returned to the States Charles was married. A silly woman, Sarah Dennis, curls, bangs, giggles . . . brainless little creature, but very pretty.

Mr. Emory died when I was thirty-eight. Before he died I had fallen in love with Charles Dennis. Absurd of me. But I was lonely, and I had no children to steady me, and Charles was a very attractive man, my dear. I think," concluded Mrs. Emory, smiling, "that he fell in love with me too. He swore he'd never been out of love with me."

You think, thought Jill, you know darned well he did, you cute old hypocrite!

Mrs. Emory laughed. She said, "Well, there were meetings and heartburnings, a few indiscreet letters and a lot of highfalutin talk. Nothing came of it, how could it? The Dennises didn't run around getting divorces, they didn't leave their wives and elope with strange or familiar women. There was a son by Charles's marriage to Sarah. I am telling you all this, partly out of vanity, which is permissible at my age, and partly to warn you that if you ever do anything to cause Charles Dennis one instant's pain I'll—I'll cut your throat," she ended belligerently.

Jill exclaimed, "You're still in love with him! Then why—?"

Mrs. Emory shook her head. She said, "Sarah's been dead only a matter of ten years or so. Disagreeable old woman she turned out to be, pains in her joints, always running to spas or taking up some newfangled religion or other. She alternated between cults and doctors. No. I—I'll admit I gave the matter some thought. But it wouldn't do at all. I am too settled in my ways and far too selfish. I wouldn't fit in. Besides, I've never had children and a stepgrandmotherly relationship to Charles's girls would have appalled me."

Jill said, "He was marvelous to me. Oh, I hope he'll like me and that I'll get on with the girls."

Mrs. Emory said, "Of course you're being overpaid. That's Charles's one weakness. He's not an extravagant man. He gives his youngsters everything, naturally, takes care of that sly little niece. But when it comes to paying people for services rendered he simply lets himself go. I have a theory that he's so ashamed to be in a position where he can pay employees that he can't bear it unless he pays too much. You know, Jill, as wages go nowadays, a job like this one of yours would usually pay about fifty a month, with board and lodging, and you'd consider yourself well off. A hundred would be generous and ample. I hope you save your salary. As for this premature bonus—for clothes, you said? That's just like him. The man's a born idiot," she decided, smiling with tenderness.

Jill said humbly, "I know. I shouldn't have taken it—or the salary either."

"Just because he's a fool," said Mrs. Emory sharply, "you needn't be one too. Take all you can get in this world. Did you meet the girls?"

"No."

"They're spoiled," said Mrs. Emory firmly. "Sally's a pretty little piece, her mother all over again in modern dress. Selfish, willful. But more to her than Sarah ever had, to my way of thinking. Mary's the odd one, can't make her out. Sally may seem to give you more trouble than Mary, but in the long run Mary will bear watching. Did you meet Elise, the niece?"

"Yes, just for a moment."

"Humph!" said Mrs. Emory, "take it you didn't like her."

"It's a little too soon to judge," Jill told her cautiously.

Mrs. Emory laughed. "You're learning," she said, pleased. "Well, it isn't too soon for me. I've known her since she was born. She's the daughter of Charles's very much younger sister, who made a bad match and died of it. Charles looks after Elise, she's lived with the family for some years. She's calculating and a snip. She won't rejoice over your coming. She would have liked the job; not that she needs the money, as Charles makes her an allowance, but—well, just for her own reasons. A little authority perhaps. She and Sally don't get on."

"Why didn't Mr. Dennis let her take charge of the younger girls?" Jill asked curiously.

Mrs. Emory frowned. "Well, there's no harm in

telling you. There was a little upset a few years ago, shortly after Elise came under Charles's guardianship: a married man . . . you know, that sort of thing . . . lots of smoke but not too much fire. Naturally Charles wouldn't be likely to give the girls into her care."

"They've had a chaperon," said Jill, "a Mrs. Peters, haven't they?"

"They ran her ragged," said Mrs. Emory with relish. "She was a gentlewoman, you know the type, black velvet and seed pearls, southern accent—she once spent three years in Virginia—and an aura of decayed gentility. No, I finally persuaded Charles that a young woman was the only possible solution . . . companion, playmate, whatever you want to term it. Of course she would have to have her head well screwed on her shoulders. I said you did. See that you don't repudiate that."

"I'm far too grateful," said Jill. "I can't properly thank you. But now I've kept you far too long."

"No!" Mrs. Emory reached out and yanked twice at a bell pull. "There'll be tea," she said firmly. "You can go shopping tomorrow. We'll let Reynolds come in and do the honors. Jill, have you ever wondered why I've kept Reynolds so long?"

"Perhaps," admitted Jill, smiling.

"Perhaps nothing. Well, I'll tell you. She's good for me. She's sour, dour, acidulous, suspicious by nature, and a complete pessimist. I'm as you know me, couldn't work up a temper if I tried, gullible as a baby in a pram. Reynolds holds me down, recalls to my wandering mind that I am but mortal and getting on in years. When she was in England and you were with me I had a very elegant time. But you were bad for me, Jill. You encouraged my extravagances, abetted my unsuitable follies. Remember the time we made the night club tour with that young man of yours, that good-looking, good-for-nothing — what's his name?"

"You mean Jimmy Bates? Yes, I remember," replied Jill, laughing, "swell, wasn't it?"

"Yes. Also you ignored my advancing years, flattered my vanity, and indulged my curiosity. It was fun, but very bad for me. Reynolds is like quinine, castor oil, and milk toast. Also sulphur and molasses."

Reynolds came, her long nose twitching with disapproval. She was suspicious of the laughter emanating from the sitting room. Tea came, and very bountiful. Reynolds turned a deaf ear to Mrs. Emory's pleas for a second cup and a third scone liberally beplastered with raspberry jam. Mrs. Emory winked her wicked black eye at Jill and looked grieved.

Jill went home in a taxi. Why not? Was she not one of the bloated rich? She hunted out Mrs. Larsen, without much difficulty, and told her she would be leaving on the first. Mrs. Larsen looked wounded but resigned. She said, with a sinister look in her currant eyes, "Very sorry, I'm sure, Miss Hamilton, and I hope you'll be very happy in your new position. Although I always say that those what eat the crumbs of the rich under the table suffers from indigestion. Perhaps," she added hopefully, "you'll be coming back to us someday."

Not if I can help it, thought Jill, but aloud she answered, "Yes, perhaps. And thank you so much, Mrs. Larsen, for all your great kindness to me."

After all, this formidable woman had been good to her. Jill resolved to buy her something, handkerchiefs, a handbag, a pair of stockings.

Fortuitously Jimmy rang her up at dinnertime and she said, "Look, the most marvelous thing has happened. Let's eat at the little French place on Sixth Avenue."

"I'm broke," said Jimmy hollowly. "Spent my last copper on stamps."

"This is on me. I've got a job and at least a million dollars. No, I can't tell you over the phone. Hurry, I'll meet you there."

"Good," said Jimmy, brightening. "I'm so hungry I could eat the hind leg of my pet wolf. I'll be right along."

Her relations with Jimmy, Jill reflected, were really quite simple and satisfactory. If she was in the money and he was not she paid the check, and the only bones he made about it were those, clean picked, of the chicken or lamb chops on his plate. Dan would be different. Dan would rather starve. He was, she thought, terribly old-fashioned. Or did one say reactionary these days? But Jimmy was casual, he shared when he had it and when he didn't he expected, or hoped, that she could do her part.

At the French place, over a very good dinner, after an unwonted and excellent cocktail, Jill made a full report. Jimmy whistled. "You are coming up in the world," he commented.

"It's fun," she told him. "Tomorrow I'm going out and drown in a sea of clothes. Look, Jimmy, I don't have to spend all the five hundred. Of course it was understood—still . . ." She reflected, her native honesty a little troubled. Then she smiled. She said, "I've forty dollars left of what I had when the job came along. Need it?"

He said, "I hate to take it, but yes, if it's all right with you. I'm sure the 'Purple Night' story will sell; it's been turned down by the best magazines and one editor wrote me a note. He said I showed promise. Whatever that means. When it does sell, I'll pay you back with interest."

"I brought it along," said Jill, and put an envelope on the table. In the morning she would cash Mr.

Dennis's check at the bank where she was known, and Mrs. Larsen was paid till the first. All Jill had to do was shop and eat until then.

Jimmy asked her about the Dennis family and she told him. He wasn't especially interested in her glowing account of its head. To young Mr. Bates a grandfather in his seventies should be kept in a glass case and taken out for an airing and permitted to sign checks once a day. He did prick up his faunlike ears, however, when she spoke of the secretary, Arden.

"What sort of bird is that?"

"Drab but smart, I'd say," replied Jill. "I didn't like him at all at first. Afterwards I wasn't so sure. I asked Mrs. Emory about him. Seems he hasn't been with Mr. Dennis very long. His former secretary, who was with him over twenty years, had to leave because of illness. Mrs. Emory doesn't seem to like the new one much. But then she's a snap-judgment sort of person."

"If he doesn't work out," suggested Jimmy, looking at her with sudden interest, "how about wangling me the job?"

"How on earth could I?" she asked, amazed.

He said, "Well, if you find he isn't too satisfactory, what's wrong with giving him a shove in the right direction and me another—provided you're strong with the old man by then? And that shouldn't be

70

hard. He may be over seventy but he still has his sight, I take it."

Jill said sharply, "I don't like that, even in fun, Jimmy. I can't go into a house and plot to get someone out of it and you in! You're wacky."

"Skip it," said Jimmy, not at all abashed, "but I'd do as much for you if I had the chance. Nowadays it's dog eat dog. Well, thanks for the dinner; it will hold me till noon. Seen your bigger and better boy friend lately?"

"Just once. He was promised a job," Jill said, "but I haven't heard from him since."

"Well, don't let it throw you. Look here, how about your free time? Do you get any, and when?"

"I don't know," said Jill; "that is, I don't know when."

"Are you permitted to have followers?" he inquired sedately, and Jill laughed.

"That's the understanding."

"Just let me know when I can call," said Jimmy. "I'll be as demure as a dove. I'll play cribbage with the old man, sing duets with the elder daughter and dress dolls with the younger. I'll give my cherished crochet patterns to the niece, and first thing you know I'll have these two old legs under the dining room table and be asking you 'Please pass the salt.' "

"Jimmy, you're impossible!"

71

He said, laughing, but she had an idea that he meant it, "I've my way to make, I detest being hungry, and a park bench would not suit my anatomy at all."

For the next few days Jill lived in a ferment of excitement. The summer clothes were in the shops, they were good enough to eat. She bought, not recklessly but carefully, buying things which, if the job didn't last, could be employed elsewhere. She assembled a wardrobe in excellent taste and with an especial charm, reflecting that if she had to leave the Dennises it would help her get other jobs. Summer clothes wouldn't be so good in Manhattan in winter, but there was always a cruise hostess chance or a Florida position. Also she had done some modeling for commercial photographers. Her especial loveliness did not lie in her features and she was exceptionally small and slight, so that it would not be likely that a model agency would keep her busy for any length of time. But there were occasional jobs, for she had had them. She had lost some because of a lack of proper wardrobe, but these clothes would be just right for summer and beach photographs. She caught herself up, thinking along these lines. Why did she always have to look ahead to the time when the old job ended and the new one began? Couldn't she get herself into the frame of mind which trusted that this one at least would be permanent? Well, not for life; but Mary

Dennis was only fourteen and it would be a good four years or more, depending on Mr. Dennis's plans, before she would be considered free to come and go as she pleased.

"I'll *make* it permanent," Jill told herself, and meant it.

CHAPTER V

On the night before she reported at the Dennis house Jill had dinner with Dan Hardy. She had not seen him since the evening at the lodging house and had told him her news over the telephone. Now, sitting opposite him in the restaurant to which he had taken her, she gave him chapter and verse, sparkling with excitement and pleasure. May being about to come in like a warm white woolly lamb, Jill had risked one of her new frocks, a "spring in town" affair, dark-navy silk, sprinkled with tiny white stars, demurely collared and cuffed, matched by a perky hat, and a thin unlined wool navy coat belted about her slim waist.

Dan listened to a rapturous narrative in which Mr. Dennis figured as elderly hero, Elise, his niece, as unknown quantity, and the secretary, Arden, as comic relief, and smiled, his dark brows raised.

"What's Arden's full name? I knew a chap once, at Tech; but no, it couldn't be."

"H. Chester Arden."

74

"Wonder why he parts his name in the middle?" murmured Dan, and Jill said laughing, "Oh, probably it's too fancy or not fancy enough." She smiled, thinking of Jimmy. Jimmy had asked the same question and they had spent a hilarious half hour thinking of names for poor bespectacled Arden . . . names ranging from Hideous and Horrible to Hara-kiri.

But Dan had forgotten H. Chester. He said, "So you're all set."

"Yes. At least," she said doubtfully, "I think so. Why?"

"Nothing. It's just that I hate to think of you . . . Jill, it is a waste of time, frittering yourself away on half a dozen little jobs."

"This isn't a little job!" she began indignantly.

"I didn't mean financially. You'll be making more than I am," he reminded her, more in astonishment than resentment, "yet I trained for a job, I know it through and through, and my education for it cost plenty, one way or another. No, not that. Really big jobs aren't necessarily the most highly paid. Look at the people in laboratories, people of whom you never hear, people living on very small salaries and content to plod along if only they may contribute something to the world, to a generation which they themselves may not live to see. As I see it, you'll be selling your wits and charm and tact shadowing a couple of spoiled

75

youngsters; and a pretty attractive duenna, if you ask me," he said, smiling at her. "You'll sing for your supper if your employer is in a receptive mood, or make a fourth at contract. It all calls for a social sense and a certain amount of intelligence. Certainly it doesn't call for prayer and fasting or the exercise of your intellect."

The pretty room seemed less attractive to Jill and the well-cooked food lost its flavor, even the new ensemble wasn't as perfect as she had thought it when she put it on. Her red hair curled softly under the little hat but her hazel-green eyes were distinctly on the green side. She said, exasperated:

"Oh, Dan, why must you be so serious about everything? If I were trained—but I'm not. I take what I can get and am glad of it. It's all experience. But you— you come along and make everything seem so futile. You place the emphasis wrongly. You'd rather I were a good housemaid, wouldn't you, working at her job? Or not working at it, and refusing to make lamp shades because lamp-shade making would be a deviation!"

He said, and the white teeth flashed, "You do make me out a pretty insufferable prig. Maybe I am. Maybe somewhere along the way I got warped. I'd like to take things lightly, catch-as-catch-can. But if you care for anything as I care for my particular profession, or perhaps if you've worked as hard as I have to be able to say such and such is my profession . . . don't sit there looking at me like that! Every hair on your head snaps at me in defiance! It's just that you're so fine, underneath all this experience veneer you've acquired, I hate to see you waste yourself."

She argued stubbornly:

"I'm not wasting myself. There is room, or should be, for a person who can do a little of everything and nothing very much!"

His face was lighted with laughter. He said, "Of course there is—you'll make someone a grand wife, someday, Jill. Certainly if there is any real market, a good, steady market, for tact and charm, it should be in marriage!"

She looked at him briefly and her eyes changed color and she felt her heart beat a little faster. She said, "I'm not ready for that job yet."

"When you are," advised Dan slowly, "be very sure that you intend it to be permanent—that you don't think, along with a lot of people in this day and age, Well, if I don't suit or it doesn't suit me, I can get out of it, I can quit and find another place!"

She asked, a little recklessly, because suddenly this room appeared to her the most delightful in the world, and the food she'd eaten the most miraculous, and the cocktail which had preceded the dinner the most courage-instilling, "You aren't proposing to me by any chance, are you, Dan?"

"No," he replied coolly, "I'm not. I think you prefer to play a lone hand. You might starve all by yourself, but I doubt if you'd starve with someone else. You'd resent that sort of starvation, wouldn't you? You can adventure alone but you don't want to adventure as half of a pair. But—since you've mentioned it—I am perfectly certain that you know I'm in love with you."

The fun had gone, the daring and the sparkle. She was ashamed and afraid. She felt the color rise, throat to temples, and she begged him, in the utmost confusion, "Please, Dan, don't. I was just being silly . . . I didn't mean . . . Oh, why," she cried, confusion giving way to irritation, "why must you be so darned *serious* about everything?"

"It is," he defended himself calmly, "the nature of the beast. Answer me truthfully. You do know, don't you?"

"No," she said, made an effort and looked at him. "No, I don't know. I mean I wasn't at all sure."

Dan asked, with extreme gravity:

"Are you in love with me?"

Not could you be, will you be, do you love me, but are you in love with me, which somehow is quite different. She looked away and was amazed at the rapidity of her pulse. She told herself scornfully, My girl, you are losing your grip, this isn't the first man who has asked you that, even if it is one of the most attractive. You must be slipping. Why all this dither and jitter? Aloud she answered:

"Dan, I don't know. I do like you, so very much. Well," she said frankly, "I think about you a lot. I get pretty excited, thinking. If you'd said anything, on the boat . . ."

"There were a lot of things I could have said," he told her, and it seemed to her that his dark eyes were somber, "but it wasn't fair to you or to myself to say any of them. I hadn't a job, about all the money I had in the world had been paid out in passage back to the States. And I'm not going to say anything now," he went on evenly, "as it wouldn't make sense. You've a job at two hundred a month. It's a job you'll hold only if you're single. I've a desk position, which isn't going to last very long . . . and I don't want it to. Even if it could last forever, I wouldn't want it. I want to get back to the work I know, and do, best. I may never make a great deal of money and I may change my job as often as you've changed yours, with this difference, they'll always be related jobs. I wouldn't ask you to chance it with me, Jill, and I've a feeling you wouldn't want to—unless you loved me a great deal. Which, my dear, you do not."

He called the waiter, consulted the menu, ordered a

sweet and coffee. Jill sat with her elbows on the table and her chin on her clasped hands and tried to believe she had heard what she had heard, tried to believe that here sat a man who announced that he was in love with her and wouldn't marry her, and apparently didn't care particularly how she felt about it. She thought on a rising tide of anger, He's perfectly right of course. I'm not in love with him. He—he just disturbs me, a little, because he's so odd and so different and so difficult. I'd be crazy to give up the Dennis offer just because he asked me— And as far as that goes, I have no choice because he didn't ask me!

Aloud she said simply:

"Dan, I think you're crazy!"

"I know I am," he agreed, smiling, "crazy about you. Which won't do me any good at all, so we're not talking about it. I shall," he announced with the utmost serenity, "get over it. At least, I can try!"

"This is the maddest conversation. Dan, you—you didn't mean it, did you?" she asked, after a moment.

"Didn't mean what?"

She was flushing again.

"Oh, any of it," she said helplessly.

"Certainly not, if you prefer it. Why?"

She said, "I'm crazy too. But I'd like us to go on being friends."

Dan Hardy flung back his dark and well-shaped head and laughed in genuine amusement. He said, "One reason I love you . . . I forgot, I mustn't say that, not if I mean it—well, then, one reason I find you very attractive is because you are an incomparable mass of contradictions. You're so terribly modern and so magnificently Victorian! Most genuinely modern young women greatly enjoy having around, when they feel like it, some poor idiot who loves them with a nice safe lack of hope and who thrives on a little encouragement. But not you. Do you really think that if I love you we can't be friends, Jill?"

She said, bright scarlet, and hating herself:

"Yes . . . no . . . that is . . . I mean—"

"Here's your bombe glacé. Eat it," he advised kindly, "and cool your fevered brow. Suppose I keep it a secret. You can ask the daisies. He loves me, he loves me not, daisies won't tell, I won't either. Not after tonight. And for heaven's sake, Jill, I take one lump and not six!"

Their waiter, finding them absorbed, had gone, and Jill was now engaged in dropping so many lumps of sugar into the tiny cup that it was in immediate danger of flooding.

They had dined early. Now the orchestra came and Dan suggested, "Let's dance. We haven't for a long time."

They danced. Once. Then Jill told him, "No more. I've got to get back and pack my things. Tomorrow's the big day, and while no one told me when I must present myself I assume it's to be bright and early."

That wasn't, of course, the reason. If to be with Dan had been exciting before this—leaning on the shiprail looking down at the dark flowing water or up at the star-lined sky, if being with him at Mrs. Larsen's, surrounded by mediocrity and bad taste, had been exciting, dancing with him tonight was dangerous. For he had told her that he loved her, and whether she believed him or not didn't matter. Her supple flesh, her young blood, her senses possessed an intelligence of their own, which had nothing to do with words, and denials and dissembling and reasoning.

She thought, If I dance with him the evening through I'll probably end by making a fool of myself and begging him to marry me at once, tomorrow, to-night. I'll end by not going to Dennis's at all. And I'm not sure that I love him! Not the least bit sure!

So she said, "Be a sweet lamb and take me home, Dan."

She was not angry at him, she was honest enough to be angry at herself. She had, through sheer bad luck or simple vanity, put herself in an impossible situation.

She slept rather badly that night. At Mrs. Larsen's

82

brownstone door Dan had said inquiringly, "I won't be seeing you, will I?" And she had checked the eager "Why not?" on her lips and replied carelessly:

"I understand that like all good domestic help I am permitted time off—which probably won't hold true in the country; but anyway," and now her recklessness and the green in her eyes returned, "I'm permitted followers" she ended with a perfectly straight face.

"You'll have them," prophesied Dan. There in the doorway he looked at her speculatively, said, with gravity and self-reproach, "I shouldn't do this!" hooked a long hard arm around her, pulled her to him, kissed her, once, hard and briefly, on the mouth, and then without further word or gesture ran down the steps and walked off.

Thinking it over afterward—and of very little else, Jill concluded that this episode was the most exciting. There she went again, using that shopworn word in connection with Dan! What made him exciting? Not his dark good looks, which weren't good looks at all but merely originality of feature, not his personality, the reverse of gay and casual—except at odd moments when he could be more casual than any human being she had hitherto encountered. That was it, his unexpectedness.

Jimmy, kissing her, was experienced and deft, had —and boasted of it—a technique. Dan had no technique at all. She didn't stop to ponder on his probable experience, she preferred not to and didn't inquire too closely into her reasons. No, he merely grabbed, kissed, and walked away.

She remembered that he hadn't told her where he was living and realized with a shock that if she had not been forehanded and provided him, at the outset of their evening together, with the Dennis name and address, they might have lost each other and never found each other again. Stranger things had happened on this little tight island, which was so big and could be so lonely, yet was always so crowded. She didn't even know the address or name of the company by which he was now employed!

She told herself severely, Jill Hamilton, you're a little moron, lying awake like this thinking about a man who says he loves you but you don't love him and that he wouldn't marry you anyway! Perhaps it's just a line. She thought of Gracie Allen and added, Perhaps he says that to all the girls! But her chuckle died aborning in her throat or else it turned into something suspiciously like a sob. You go to sleep, she ordered, or else you'll look like a hag in the morning and you'll be fired without a month's notice and Mr. Dennis will say, Young woman, where is that five hundred dollars? I gave it to a nice little girl with red hair and green eyes, not to Farmer Brown's most effective scare-

84

crow. A sudden horrifying thought struck her and she sat up in bed, clasping her hands about her knees. "What if he'd take back the clothes?" she inquired aloud and, overcome by this grim possibility, sank back on the pillow with a low moan and almost instantly fell asleep.

On May 1st, as it was May Day, she presented herself at nine o'clock at the Dennis door, looking like a basket of flowers, very fresh and crisp and charming. The taxi man carried her brand-new suitcase and hatbox and delivered them to the ancient butler whose name Jill immediately ascertained was Joseph. After which a bell was pressed and a brawny young houseman appeared to assist the taxi driver with Jill's equally new trunk.

Mr. Arden appeared, his nondescript hair brushed and shining and his spectacles gleaming with a special polish which Jill hoped was of welcome. He made her a curious little speech, which appeared half inevitable formality and half genuine friendliness, and presented her to Mrs. Gadman, commonly called Gadget, as Jill afterward learned. Mrs. Gadman was the housekeeper. She had been Mary and Sally's nurse and that of their mother before them. She was old, stooped, gray, thin as a wisp, and gentle as a dove. It was she who took Jill to her room and explained that the young ladies

85

had gone to school, Mr. Dennis was downtown on business, and Miss Elise was not yet up.

The house was bigger than it looked from the outside, and ascending in the little self-operating elevator to the third floor Gadget explained to Jill that Mr. Dennis's suite was on the second floor, as was Mr. Arden's room. On the third Sally and Mary had their quarters, two bedrooms, a little living room, and a shared bath. There was Elise's room and bath, Jill's, and a guest room. On the fourth floor, the domestic service staff. The houseman "slept out," Gadget said, while the family were in the city. Living in were herself, Joseph, the cook, and the chambermaid.

Jill's room was small, comfortable, and quite delightful, comprising rosy walls, and turquoise blue draperies, small, deep chairs, a three-quarter bed, bookshelves, ample closet space, an extension telephone, and a secretary-desk.

Gadget in her neat black silk watched Jill look around and smiled pleasantly. She said, "I hope you'll be very happy here, Miss Hamilton," and Jill, repressing a desire to throw her arms around the little woman's neck, answered, "I'm sure I shall be," sedately enough, but her eyes danced.

She had most of the day in which to unpack. She saw Elise at luncheontime, but Elise was going out and stopped merely to nod casually en route to the door. Mr. Dennis had not returned and Jill and H. Chester Arden lunched alone, in the lovely dining room, meticulously served by Joseph. Luncheon was simple and very good, and Mr. Arden smiled at Jill across the sea of wine-dark mahogany. There was a certain domesticity about the little meal which did not escape him and which vaguely pleased him. Of course H. Chester had ambitions, he didn't intend to indulge in interludes with another, and inferior, employee of Dennis's. He had other plans. However, Jill was pretty and amusing and it wouldn't be half bad to have her around. His own personal taste ran to more flamboyant blonds, with softer eyes and the minimum of brains, but meantime it wasn't a bad idea to cultivate the friendship of an attractive little person whom one could, undoubtedly, impress.

The girls, he told Jill, lunched at their school. They would be home shortly after four. He expected Mr. Dennis in by teatime.

After luncheon, although it was patent that Mr. Arden expected her to linger, Jill escaped and went upstairs to write to Jimmy and to Helen Elliott. To the latter she wrote in part: "This is a pretty elegant setup. I think I'll get along with Gadget and Joseph all right. They're the real thing . . . like an English novel. I keep looking for the green baize door to the kitchen quarters but I suppose there isn't any. I haven't laid eyes on my charges yet and am wondering if I have to call them Miss Dennis—separately of course—or if I'll be permitted the use of Christian names. As for H. Chester, I'm not at all sure about him. When are you returning, be sure to write me, call me up when you reach town." She gave Helen the Dennis private number, leaning over to read it on the telephone. Then she dropped her pen and made an untidy blot. If Dan hadn't kept that slip of paper with the Dennis address on it he'd never find her, not certainly in the phone book.

There were brightly jacketed new novels on her bookshelves and presently she settled to one of them in the most comfortable chair. Around four o'clock the small house telephone on the shelf rang and Jill jumped up wildly, answered the extension, was greeted by "Number, please?" and then finally located the house instrument.

It was Arden, brisk and competent. Mr. Dennis had returned, and would Miss Hamilton join him for tea in the library?

Jill dropped her book, rushed to the mirror, did the necessary things and scorning the elevator ran down the two flights to the library floor. Joseph opened the door for her and Mr. Dennis rose from behind his desk.

88

He said, smiling, "I'm glad to see you. Tell me, are you quite comfortable in your new quarters?"

"Not only comfortable but luxurious," Jill told him. Arden was not in the room so she went on hesitantly, "I—I want to thank you for your very great generosity to me, Mr. Dennis. I wrote you, but I wanted to tell you how grateful I am."

"It was a nice little note," he said, smiling. "Sit down at the tea table, Jill. You don't mind if I call you that? This is not a formal household although my very efficient secretary tries to make it so," he added, twinkling, "and I need not tell you how deeply I hope you will be content with us. The girls will be in presently. Would you," he asked her, "pour tea? You might as well know now as later that I take it strong, with three lumps of sugar and plenty of cream."

Jill poured, lifting the heavy silver pot. The china was Sèvres, delicate and colorful, and the old spoons were worn very thin. There was cinnamon toast and dripping crumpets, and she sighed aloud, "I'll put on weight!"

"You can afford to. I don't approve of this modern mania of overslenderness," said her employer. "Mary, bless her, worries me considerably by trying to lose weight. I keep assuring her it's merely puppy fat but the term neither convinces nor appeals to her. How much do you weigh?"

"A hundred and five."

He said calmly, "We'll put ten pounds on you in no time."

"Oh," cried Jill, "I hope not! All my lovely new clothes!"

"Mrs. Gadman is an excellent seamstress," said Dennis mildly. "Tell me something about yourself. Mrs. Emory says you have a fund of hair-raising yarns."

They were laughing together when Arden came in for his tea, Jill having just recounted one of her more outrageous and amusing experiences. "This little girl," chuckled Mr. Dennis to his secretary, "is extremely resourceful. Has she told you about the snake charmer and the living skeleton?"

H. Chester raised an almost invisible eyebrow and replied, "No, unfortunately," and Jill resolved to tell him at the first opportunity, it being perfectly obvious that never in his life had Mr. Arden had any truck with snake charmers or living skeletons, even at second hand and by hearsay.

Elise came in. A silver fox lay over one printed silk shoulder and she looked bored and tired. She glanced fleetingly at Jill behind the tea table, her expression perfectly readable. Jill asked, "Tea, Miss Henshaw?" and when Elise, looking not at her but at Arden, said, yawning, "Ring for Joseph, will you, Chester, and ask him for some iced tea instead?" Jill felt her color rise.

She said disarmingly:

"As you weren't here I thought I'd substitute for you . . ." And was rewarded by Elise's patronizing smile. As a matter of fact, Elise disliked pouring daily tea. It smacked of duty and meant being on time. But she had resented Jill's place behind the low round table. As long as Jill had the common sense to recognize that it wasn't her place, thought Elise, she could pour till doomsday and welcome.

Charles Dennis had become in the course of the years a rather unworldly gentleman but he still recognized strategy when he saw it. Jill's rising inflection at the end of her sentence had been a minor masterpiece. He suppressed a slight smile and Arden, who had long felt that his was the corner on diplomacy, experienced some uneasiness.

Sally and Mary came in without ceremony. Elise, sunk in a tall chair with her iced tea beside her, waved to them languidly and they went over to kiss their grandfather . . . a gesture which struck Jill as being a daily ceremony. Mr. Dennis made the necessary introductions and Jill shook hands with her new responsibilities and suffered their appraising eyes smilingly.

Sally was tall and slender, with flyaway yellow hair and the bright blue Dennis eyes. She looked a very little like Elise but with much more color and life. She was pleasant to Jill, but beneath it Jill sensed a rather definite hostility. Mary, on the other hand, was frankly sullen, and Jill preferred it. Much better to know what you face, she thought. Mary was tall for her age, and very nearly fat. Lumpy at best. She had brown hair, dark eyes, and features more or less obscured by the roundness of her face. She said, "Hello," jerkily, and escaped to sit on her grandfather's knee.

Elise watched, smiling from her corner; Arden watched too, and Jill felt like some sort of animal that is being put through its paces under all those watching eyes. Only those of Charles Dennis were friendly, without reservations.

CHAPTER VI

FOR the next few weeks, until the Dennises moved to Long Island, Jill considered honestly that she didn't earn her salt, much less her afternoon tea and two hundred a month. She drove with the girls to school, to Mary's obvious resentment, and she called for them. She took them to a movie they wanted to see and to the dentist's and the doctor's for their spring going-over. She shopped with them on Saturdays for their summer things, the tacit understanding being that while they were old enough to know what they wanted they must be gently guided in their choice.

Mary, Jill discovered, had little interest in clothes. Someone had told the child that no amount of dressing would improve her appearance, therefore she hated shops, was sullen and ill at ease, patently uninterested, bored and fidgety at fittings. By the second excursion Jill had learned how to handle her. She suggested tailored cool summer frocks for daytime wear, steered tactfully away from shorts, bought dark, good-looking riding clothes for her, and after much patient searching found suits and dressier afternoon and simple evening things which had lines that were flattering to the child's outsize and overgrown figure. Sally of course looked like a dream in anything she put on, but Jill discovered that her courteous attention and acquiescence cloaked a far more stubborn will than Mary's open hostility. Sally at seventeen wanted what most seventeen-year-old girls had, whether their parents approved or not, she wanted evening frocks which were, in her own phrase, "sophisticated" and which meant mostly naked, she wanted plentiful lipstick and funny hair-dos, and all the rest of it. Normally Jill wouldn't have paid much attention. Seventeen-year-old girls these days were considered fully adult. But Mr. Dennis had had a little talk with her.

"I don't want to be severe with Sally," he said wistfully, "and I assume from observation and reading that girls her age are considerably more free than they used to be. But if you could steer her away from blatant paint and haystack curls and gowns which in my youth I remember seeing chorus girls wearing . . . She's so very young, Jill. I'd like to keep her so for a little while. She has all her life before her in which to grow old."

With this in mind Jill concentrated on Sally's education. She pointed out how much more "sophisticated" simplicity was, how much more alluring an adequate amount of covering than crass exposure. She talked busily of the vogue for an even smooth tan and how it called for very little powder, no rouge, and the minimum of lipstick. She looked up fashion magazines carrying articles which bore her out, and left them around so that Sally would be sure to see them. And she prattled artlessly about the new mode of naturalness which, she assured her listener, was taking hold in Hollywood. All this had the desired result of guiding Miss Sally to really charming and becoming summer things at which her grandfather would be unable to raise his eyebrows.

The first-name stage had been easily reached. Mr. Dennis had called her Jill from the beginning and Mary was the next to follow him. Her hostility was only a veneer of suspicion. She was afraid of being laughed at, she had all the delicate terrors, the heartbreaking anxieties of adolescence and she suffered because of Sally's seniority and good looks. She, Mary, was plain and fat and therefore would rather be dead, or so she exclaimed passionately to Jill one hot May evening, when wandering into Jill's room she found her writing letters.

"You aren't plain," denied Jill calmly, surveying her. "You have very fine eyes and eyebrows. Don't pluck them, Mary; that takes all the character away from your face. You have good teeth. And you'll have a good skin when you stop smearing it with all sorts of creams which won't do it any good until you start working at it from the inside out . . . diet, water, air, exercise, sleep. You'll be amazed at the result and then you can use all your beloved creams with impunity. As for being fat, part of it's your age and part of it's laziness, too many sodas and too many boxes of candy. You can diet without starving to death, you know, and it's worth it. When you are Sally's age you'll be very pretty."

"Oh, Jill!" cried Mary with a little gasp of pure rapture. Then she added timidly, "Do you mind if I call you that?"

"No," said Jill, "I don't. I like it." She looked at the fat little girl with a twinkle of pure amusement.

"Don't worry, Mary," she said, "you'll be a knock-out one of these days. And moreover you won't have to rely just on your looks. You like to read, you're intelligent. You'll have just what it takes," went on Jill serenely, conscious that her phraseology might be reprehensible when lecturing the young, but at least it was a language the young could understand, "so don't worry about now—this minute—today." She tilted her red head and looked a trifle secretive and rather wicked. "Besides," she added, "you'll have more fun when you're older. Even if you were a fourteen-year-old Shirley Temple at this minute, what good would it do you? Just between us," Jill concluded, slightly alarmed at her own unorthodox way of teaching the young idea to shoot, "boys wouldn't play much part in your life at present."

"I hate 'em," said Mary with a return to her sullenness.

"Oh, no, you don't," contradicted Jill. "You just think you do because you're afraid they won't like you."

"That's mean," Mary announced, and regarded Jill with deep resentment. "It isn't my fault if they don't like me. You saw how it was at dancing school last week."

Jill nodded. She had taken Mary to dancing school and stayed there with her. Most of Mary's dances were claimed by the dapper, ancient instructor. Jill said, smiling:

"Don't get sore. They'll like you all right—at the proper time. Now it wouldn't make sense. The older boys wouldn't have much use for you anyway, even if you were slender as Sally, and the younger ones would bore you to distraction. But in a few years everything will be very different. You wait and see! But don't wait with your hands folded. Do something about it . . . work for what you want, no one ever got anything without working."

"Sally does," said Mary, quivering.

"Do you remember Sally a few years ago, Mary, when she was thirteen or fourteen?"

"Of course I do. Of all the mean, nasty—!"

"Wait a minute. What did she look like?"

"Oh," said Mary, "she was thin, her feet and hands were too big and she wore braces—like I'm wearing now—on her front teeth."

"Well," said Jill triumphantly, "Sally worked, didn't she? And time made a difference. You're just proving it to me. Of course there must be material with which to work. Sally had. So have you. And I recommend that you do a little thinking about exercise and diet, soap and water. I'll help you all I can. Is it a bargain . . . just between us two?"

"Oh," cried Mary in an ecstasy of excitement and gratitude, "you're such a darling, Jill." She flung herself across the room and embraced Jill, nearly knocking her out of her chair, disheveling her hair and practically breaking her neck. Jill bore it like a martyr, without a murmur. "Sally and Elise—I detest Elise, she reminds me of a faded snake—" said Mary vehemently, "they say you're calculating and want to worm your way into Grandfather's good graces."

"Mary, keep still," began Jill firmly, but Mary in full spate did not even hear her but went on wildly:

"And Elise said she wouldn't be a bit surprised if you were trying to marry Grandfather. That's very silly because he's an old man," she commented disdainfully; "anyway I don't believe a word of it. I do like you, Jill, I think you're perfectly swell."

So that's what they think, is it? thought Jill with an uprush of anger. Aloud she said, "That's fine, Mary, I like you too. Run along now like a good girl, I must finish my letters."

When Mary had departed, knocking into a bedside table, falling over her feet, and slamming the door lustily, Jill chewed her pen and considered. She thought, Well, darn 'em anyway! If I had an ounce of proper pride I'd up and quit this instant minute. I haven't the ounce, it seems, she went on thoughtfully, because I'm so mad I'll stay till doomsday if only to prove they're wrong. Brats, she thought, including Elise in the term. Well, I've one friend at court anyway! Mrs. Emory, bless her heart, was all wrong about the girls. All Mary needs is to lose twenty-odd pounds and gain confidence. She isn't the one who'll bear watching. But Sally!

She shook her red head and settled down to finish her letter to Jimmy. She had seen him two or three times since coming to the Dennises'. He was, unfortunately, free mornings, and after Jill had taken the girls to school she had practically nothing to do until they returned again.

She had not seen Dan at all, but he had written her.

She left his letter until the last, pondering over her reply, tearing up sheet after sheet, trying to infuse the written words with just the right, light touch. He had kept her address, it appeared, but wrote that her Mr. Dennis must be, at least, the Queen of Spain, as it was impossible to coax the telephone number out of the operator. And could she have dinner with him before she went away? He had something to tell her.

Jill procured time off without any difficulty and went out to dine with Dan a few days before she left for Long Island. She had a good deal to tell him about her platinum-lined job. Was she, he inquired, happy in it? Jill, nodding vigorously, assured him that she was. She said:

"I'm not entirely accepted. H. Chester looks at me with some misgiving and Elise doesn't like me at all. They call me Jill. I retaliate with Mr. Arden and Miss Henshaw. They approve of that, it puts me in my place. I've won a firm friend in Mary. Just at present she adores me, hangs on my lightest word. Sally is polite. That's about all. She doesn't in the least adore me, thinks she's far too old to have me tagging around and perhaps she is, I don't know. She has a rather nice little voice and I've played her accompaniments once or twice. Oh, we get along . . . perhaps we'll do better in the country."

"That's what I wanted to talk to you about. Where is the Dennis place?"

She told him, regarding him inquiringly. And Dan said, "Well, you'll be seein' me."

"Dan, what do you mean? What happened to your job?"

"Oh, I didn't mean I'd turn up asking for a place as undergardener," he assured her, "but there's a new road going through your district down there, complete with ramps and landscaping and State Police quarters, one of the last links in the chain. It's a Federal affair, and through a political gentleman who seems to be fingering a lot of pies, I've the job of seeing it through. I begin next month. How long it will last I have no idea but it's good work and interests me very much. I won't be living far away and perhaps if you're a very good girl your boss will let me come and call at the back gate now and then."

"Dan, that's perfectly wonderful!" she exclaimed and showed him such starry eyes that he looked at her gravely and shook his head.

"None of your wiles, woman," he said sternly.

"I wasn't wiling," she told him with indignation. "I'm just glad, that's all."

"Seen your little friend Jimmy of late?" inquired Dan.

She was a little disconcerted by the change of subject but rallied bravely.

"Oh, a couple of times. He's coming to tea the day before we leave. It appears that I may have guests for tea. Too bad," she added, "that your hours don't permit."

"And Jimmy's do?"

"Well, frankly," said Jill laughing, "he doesn't seem to have hours."

Jimmy came to tea duly and ingratiated himself with Mr. Dennis, Elise, and the two girls. Elise, Jill noticed from behind the tea service, regarded him with interest and exhibited her special slow smile for him at intervals. Mr. Dennis frankly enjoyed him, and he was attentive to both youngsters. Sally tossed her flyaway curls and preened and even Mary came out of her shell. Only H. Chester Arden, sitting in a corner like Jack Horner, put in his thumb now and then and if what he pulled out was a plum he looked at it with distaste. It was evident that Jimmy was too frivolous for H. Chester.

At dinner that night Mr. Dennis spoke of "your young man" to Jill. Jill, disclaiming all possession, shook her head.

"He isn't at all, Mr. Dennis, just a good friend. I've known him a long time. We like each other," she explained with her disarming smile, "and we've had a good deal of fun together."

Arden murmured something that sounded like "lightweight" and Elise looked over at Jill sharply. Jill went on:

"He's had rather hard luck lately. At college he majored in English Literature. He wanted to write, after he'd had postgraduate work and travel. I think he has a gift, although of course I'm not much of a judge. Then he wasn't able to go on with his studies and, as he hadn't trained for anything special, he's held all sorts of odd jobs since, most of them brief. He's very gay about it and lighthearted, but I do think underneath he feels keenly that he hasn't established himself. He has to eat, after all, and when you don't sell . . . He has sold some minor things but not enough to keep him out of a steady job . . . if he could get one."

H. Chester fixed her with a stern eye.

"Is he of the Hemingway or Faulkner school?" he inquired darkly.

Jill laughed.

"I haven't the least idea," she answered and then, struck with a brilliant idea, turned a winning smile toward Mr. Arden, "but I'm sure," she said, "that you are something of a critic. You could help Jimmy a lot. Of course he knows writers, but the majority of them are poor and struggling like himself. Some have other jobs. Most haven't anything. They belong to the sit-around-and-talk-about-it school," explained Jill, as Mr. Dennis chuckled, "and they can't help Jimmy much. But I am sure you could if you would have the time and patience to read some of his things someday," she concluded admiringly.

Next to curiosity, vanity was Mr. Arden's besetting sin, and he relaxed.

"I would be very glad to," he said graciously and then shot her a look of extreme caution and speculation through his shining lenses. He wasn't, as it happened, particularly dumb.

Jimmy, Jill reflected, had been a model of propriety during that tea hour. He did not come too early or too late nor did he stay too long. Toward Jill he had behaved as an old friend, one who regarded her with fraternal affection. As this was an attitude which she certainly had not encountered in him hitherto, Jill was, not unnaturally, impressed.

She had, however, accompanied him to the hallway when he took his departure and he had there seized her hands in a far from fraternal grip.

"You're sitting pretty, darling," he had murmured, "and there's a place for me. I'm sure of it. Give Arden a kick in the pants for me, will you, and hasten his departure. By the way, you aren't the woman I took you for if you can't find out what the H stands for. I've had several excellent ideas on the matter since I saw you last: Helot, a good old crossword puzzle name for slave, and some others I haven't time to go into just now. 'Bye, be seein' you soon."

"Not till fall," she said sadly.

"Don't count on that, Toots," said Jimmy gaily. "Or didn't you hear Mr. Dennis say, 'Perhaps sometime you will come and spend a weekend with us. We want Jill to feel that she is free to have her own guests, you know'?"

"Jimmy! I hope you refused!"

"Have I gone nerts? I accepted. And I won't let him or you forget that. Farewell, and if it be forever—but it won't be. Consider yourself bussed. Adiós."

Jimmy, reflected Jill, was impossible. And great fun.

The exodus to Long Island was accomplished with little fret and fever, by means of automobiles and trains. Gadget went on ahead to see that everything was in order. The cook, chambermaid, and Joseph departed in one car right after luncheon and were driven by Frank, the handy man. The family went down in the big car with the chauffeur, all except Arden, who drove his own small car.

The place was on the north side of the Island. It was called, without much imagination, Shoreglen, and was really very attractive. There were over fifty acres, a sandy white beach, a dock and a boathouse. The house itself was comfortable and hideous after the fashion of architecture fifty or sixty years ago. It was frame, large, three stories, sprawling, with mansard roofs and a porte-cochere, great porches, with bright rugs and furniture, hardwood floors, paneling, adequate bathrooms recently modernized, a big billiard room, and, it seemed to the bewildered Jill, at least forty bedrooms.

The domestic staff was considerably augmented by in-servants and the outside string of superintendent and gardeners. The gardens were lovely, formal and informal, with miles of hedges, cutting gardens, and rose gardens. The lawns were close clipped, velvet smooth, and there were fine old trees. Part of the place was in farm land, there were horses and cows in the stables and chickens and turkeys in the poultry yards. And a kitchen garden which supplied the table.

The Dennises, Jill decided, lived as well as anyone she had ever known. She had once been employed for a short time as a confidential secretary—letters written by hand—by a very rich woman, in Westchester. She had selected Jill for her penmanship, her looks, and her voice over the telephone. That estate had been far larger and more formal, replete with butlers and footmen and half a dozen cars and all the most modern contraptions in and out of the house. But even Mrs.

Hinckman's vast possessions—Chinese room, Victorian room, library of twenty thousand books, two swimming pools, beach houses and guest cottages—hadn't given Jill the sense of comfort, luxury without ostentation, and money without emphasis that Shoreglen did.

She settled quickly into the routine of the house. She swam with the girls, rode with them, played tennis with them, hiked with Mary and kept her eye on her younger charge's diet. She went with them to several garden and dancing parties during that first month and acquitted herself as their unofficial hostess. The place was always full of young people and there were weekend guests, generally Sally's friends, and youngsters for lunch and dinner and tea.

H. Chester, in the country, astonished her. He seemed a great deal more human. He played an excellent game of tennis and swam very well. And as time went on and July came in, blazing hot, with scarcely a breath of air under the trees, and their activities lessened, he spent a good deal of time with Jill. Mr. Dennis was working on a book but the heat told on him and for a week or so he shortened his hours and lay about in a lawn chair under the trees, reading, watched the tennis which Mary played in the cooler evening, or the swimming. Which left H. Chester rather free.

One day lying out on the raft, trailing a pink toe

in the blue waters of the Sound, Jill, beautifully tanned and very pretty in her brief green suit, asked him, not as idly as it sounded:

"Would you tell me something?"

"Of course."

Without his spectacles H. Chester was much more personable. He beamed on her almost fraternally. She thought him something of a horror in his bathing suit as he was certainly very thin, and very knobby, and averting her eyes replied, meekly:

"You'll think me very curious. But . . . it's your first name. What does the H stand for?"

He said, and laughed suddenly, looking much younger and more attractive:

"Have you tried to guess?"

"I'm afraid so."

"And have you arrived at any conclusion?"

"Well, Henry, Howard, Harry, Harcourt—and of course," she said solemnly, "Handsome and Hernest."

"What?"

"Hernest. It's very British."

Mr. Arden smiled. He said, and looked at her slim curves with obvious approval:

"I tell very few people. Will you promise me that it will remain a secret?"

Jill crossed her fingers and murmured fervently, "I

promise." But she made reservations . . . Dan and Jimmy. They didn't count.

"Heronimus!"

Without a sound, until she splashed, Jill rolled off the raft.

When she came up again, her brown face glistening, and smiled at him, clinging to the edge of the raft, Arden reached over, and with surprising strength caught her hands and helped her clamber up without benefit of steps. He said sadly:

"Pretty bad, isn't it?"

"I think it's grand," she said. She laughed all over her little face. And then, because the day was so clear and fine, the water so exhilarating and her job such fun, she mourned, "But I can't call you that!"

He said, "Chester's all right. I've been waiting."

Dressing, Jill told herself in some amazement, I believe he's loosening up. Perhaps I hastened it a little. Perhaps it was a mistake. I don't know. Heronimus! Wait till Jimmy hears that!

He wouldn't have to wait long. He had managed what Jill believed to be impossible—the invitation to Shoreglen. She had had no intention of asking him, of securing permission to ask him. His plaintive letters to her would, naturally, never reach Mr. Dennis's eyes. But Jimmy was too clever for her. He had spent a good deal of time in secondhand bookstores, after his teatime call. For during his hour under the Dennis roof he had heard his host mention an old book which his booksellers had not been able to procure for him. It was a history of one of New York State's counties, long out of print. Jimmy, searching assiduously, had turned it up, had put a deposit of two dollars on it, beaten the obscure bookseller down from seven dollars to five, borrowed three from a temporarily solvent friend and sent it off to Long Island with a graceful little note.

The result was to be expected. Mr. Dennis was charmed at such consideration in one so young. He came, beaming all over, to Jill, the book in one hand and the letter in the other. "Delightful young man," he said. "Jill, why don't you ask him down?"

She had a thousand excuses on the tip of her tongue, there were other guests, she didn't wish to impose—

"Nonsense," he said. He smiled affectionately at her. "Can't I ever persuade you to consider yourself at home here? Ask him by all means."

She did so, with misgivings, and Jimmy drove down the following week in a battered car which he had borrowed from a friend. He had a new bathing suit and an old tennis racquet and his white flannels were shrunken and his pull-overs full of holes. But he was utterly unapologetic, which endeared him to his host; his two new shirts were pristine . . . and his blue coat not so bad. He stayed the weekend, devoted himself to Mr. Dennis, to Arden's annoyance, and was so charming to Mary that she suffered all the thrilling and pleasant throes of her first crush. He golfed with Elise, played tennis with Sally, and was brotherly toward Jill. And departed when his weekend was over, secure in the knowledge that Dennis had asked him to come back, any time. "Just ring us up," he said cordially, "we can always fit you in."

Jill was a little dashed by Jimmy's neglect of her and more than a little irritated by the reason for it. He had confided it to her one day on the beach, during a swim. He hugged his knees, looked out across the water and said calmly, "Of course, my angel, you will realize that I pay no attention to you whatever. But there are reasons. Your friend Elise is one. She would resent attention to anyone but herself. And she has her uncle's ear. Likewise it is diplomatic to be attentive to one's host. Later, when I have established my footing more firmly, I'll make up for lost time. I loathe wasting moonlight and roses but—well, wait and see. You'll not suffer by it."

She said indignantly, "I'm not suffering now. And I think you're the absolute pay-off, Jimmy Bates. Of all the cold-blooded, calculating . . ."

"Hush," he said gently, "you deeply wrong me." He waved a hand at Sally picking her way across the sand. "Race you to the raft, young lady," he challenged her.

On Monday he had gone and everyone missed him and admitted it, except Jill. She didn't miss him, she told herself crossly, he was the limit . . . all he wanted was free meals, a comfortable bed, and entertainment without paying for it. He made her sick. But it was dull without him.

That Monday night there was the moon which Jimmy had deplored as wasted. Mary was early in bed with a slight cold and Sally had a school friend visiting her. Elise had gone out and Mr. Dennis was reading in the library. Jill, going out on the porch for a breath of air and a glimpse of the roses drenched in silver and of the water beyond, was startled when Arden rose from a swing near by.

"I was thinking of you," he said, "sit down here with me, won't you?"

She said, "Just for a minute. I have to look in on Mary and I've got to see that Sally and the Hill girl don't slip away from under my nose for moonlight bathing. It's all right for Sally, but the Hill child doesn't swim well enough and is the most obstinate little thing."

"You're doing awfully well with the girls," he complimented her, "much better than I had expected."

She said, sinking back against the cushions beside

him and looking out over lawns and gardens and water, "Isn't it marvelous tonight? Fireflies as big as lanterns. Oh, well, I don't know," she replied doubtfully, "I've thinned Mary down a bit—I do think she looks well, don't you? All she needed was someone to encourage her—but Sally doesn't like me."

"Doesn't she? I don't see how she could help it. I tried not to," admitted Mr. Arden.

It came without warning, the arm about her, the sudden embrace, the warm breath on her cheek, the swift and not at all clumsy kiss.

"You do get under one's skin," murmured Mr. Arden pleasantly, "and I think we're a good deal alike."

Jill drew away, not hastily but deftly. She thought, Here's a pretty kettle of finny denizens. If I get sore, then he'll make trouble for me; if I don't, he'll make trouble for me too.

She said lightly, "Chester, the moonlight has gone to your head. How are we alike?"

He said, "Opportunists. And this is one opportunity I'd be a fool to neglect. Has it never occurred to you, Jill, that we might have a very amusing time together? No one need know about it, naturally. It can be arranged. After all, you know all the answers, and it is pretty boring day in and day out, surrounded by youngsters and bores. But if one had a secret diversion?" He added, "I don't expect to marry, you know, for a good many years. I had," he went on, insufferably frank, "thought of Sally. But she is very young. And before she is of the proper age I won't be here. I hope I won't be here much longer. But you are a sophisticated person, you've been around, you know what it's all about. And I flatter myself you like me a little, don't you?"

CHAPTER VII

Jill was silent for a full half minute, a reaction not altogether displeasing to H. Chester, who flattered himself that she was overcome by the proposed honor or speechless with maidenly confusion. He could not know that she was struggling with herself, arguing that an outburst at this period was not indicated. If she slapped his silly face, if she said, roundly, "you idiotic little beast," it wouldn't do her much good, she reflected. She would only make a rather powerful enemy, and she had a sudden, sure intuition that H. Chester could make things very unpleasant for her if he wished.

Certainly, she could go to Mr. Dennis and complain of his secretary's extraordinary behavior and she was sure that H. Chester would be set none too gently on the carpet. But Mr. Dennis had known Arden longer than he had known Jill and it was quite plausible that the young man would have all kinds of excuses, including the original one, the infallible precedent which begins, "And the woman tempted me . . ."

No, it would not be wise to antagonize H. Chester too much, or at least not quite now. She would have to wait until she was more firmly established in the Dennis household. Meantime, she thought, she could handle this astonishing worm who had turned, and with a vengeance. She was not completely aware that Arden's stilted manner, his pedantry, his gravity, all probably entirely natural to him and not acquired, served him as a rather neat disguise.

"Well?" he inquired, breaking the silence.

Jill emitted what can only be termed a girlish giggle. She didn't dare exclaim, "But, Heronimus, this is so sudden," much as she would have liked to do so. Now that her first flare of hot anger had passed, the situation had begun to amuse her. It called for all her wits, and she had grown accustomed to exercise these in the last crowded years. She reflected briefly that for a girl not placed as she was the situation admitted of but one straightforward course. But she could not stop to think about that fortunate and hypothetical creature, she had to accept things as they were.

She said, "Of course I like you—Chester. Lots. But you're pretty overwhelming, you know."

She was a little anxious, waiting, but her anxiety passed as he replied smugly:

"Perhaps I am. I admit that I don't often permit

myself the luxury of impulse, but when I do I am quite carried away, as you have seen."

She said coaxingly:

"But even you can't rush a girl into—into something serious. And perhaps it's the moonlight. You'll feel differently tomorrow. After all, we'll be together a long time—I hope. And, well, we don't know each other very well, Chester, do we, and you'd be terribly annoyed with yourself if you decided in a day or two that you hadn't meant what you said and were more or less committed?"

Good heavens, thought H. Chester, in a tumult, she is taking this seriously! After all I said about not marrying for a number of years, is it possible that she believed her charms had overthrown my scruples?

He was distressed and somewhat worried but not at all angry. He came to the conclusion that possibly Jill wasn't quite the sophisticate he had imagined her. And she'd take a bit of winning. He wasn't exactly displeased at the thought. He put his arm about her again, lightly, and said:

"I didn't mean to frighten you."

Jill stiffened imperceptibly under his clasp. So the imbecile thought her frightened, did he? That showed how much he knew about her! She had fought her way out of even worse situations than this one, with tact, her native wit, and more than a hint of permissible feminine deceit as her only weapons.

They both heard the clatter of heels on the wooden flooring of the porch, and H. Chester, without haste but in time, withdrew his offending and offensive arm, sat back and lit a cigarette with steady fingers. Jill, looking up, was as glad to see one of the maids round the porch corner and come toward them as she would have been to see the Charge of the Light Brigade bearing down on her in full cry, intent on rescue.

"Miss Hamilton?" asked the girl hesitantly, peering into the darkened corner.

"I'm here, Jane," answered Jill, "someone looking for me?"

"It's Mr. Dennis, miss. There's a caller come . . . they're in the library."

Jill rose. She murmured an apology to H. Chester, and supplemented it by a "Seems as if I were summoned, darn it," with just the proper amount of reluctance. H. Chester sighed, "Get away as soon as you can," he commanded, when the maid was out of earshot.

Jill, making her way back into the house, thought grimly, And that's that. I'll have to keep myself in daylight after this when he's around. It would be, she knew, pretty difficult to avoid him. The old game of stalling was the best until she felt the ground firm under her feet and could afford to do and say all the things she felt like doing and saying. She found time to be a little sorry for herself. Heaven knew she hadn't invited this visitation, she'd only wanted to be friendly with her fellow employee—friendliness seemed indicated if you had to live under the same roof as other people. And look what it had got her into!

She knocked at the library door and Charles Dennis told her to come in. Opening the door she stood transfixed with astonishment on the threshold, for there, rising from one of the biggest chairs, one of Mr. Dennis's excellent cigars smoldering between his fingers, was the last person she expected to see.

"Why, Dan Hardy!" she said in amazement.

He took her hands, swung them, looked her over from top to toe. "The country agrees with you," he said.

Mr. Dennis beamed upon them mildly and Jill turned on him for an explanation.

"How on earth did you get here?" she demanded.

But Dan spoke for himself.

"Been down quite a few days," he informed her, "but haven't had much time on my hands, even at night. Found a place to board, not half a mile away, and walked up tonight thinking perhaps you'd be in. I understand," he told Mr. Dennis gravely, "that Jill is permitted followers. Those were her very words, I take them at their face value."

Charles Dennis laughed. He said:

"We have no idea of cutting her off from her friends and when one of them happens to be the son of a friend of mine—"

Jill looked from one to the other, wide-eyed, and Mr. Dennis went on:

"I happened to be in the hall when Mr. Hardy arrived, and asked him in and sent Jane looking for you. She took quite a time to locate you and meantime we came back here and had a pleasant talk. When I was a youngster I spent some years in Pennsylvania with relatives . . . my parents were dead, and I had been provided with a plethora of guardians. During that Pennsylvania period I attended the high school in the town and my closest friend was Richard Hardy—what happened to your Uncle Dick?" he asked Dan suddenly.

"Spanish-American War," Dan replied. "I never knew him."

"No, of course not. Well, I used to go to Dick's house and a most hospitable place it was, with half a dozen other youngsters there, one of whom became this young man's father, then a sturdy youngster of about six. He used to go fishing with us, no amount of persuasion could shake him off. He was a great kid, and I have always remembered him, a persistent and solemn young person and a very good sport. I led a very idyllic existence for several years in that sleepy Pennsylvania Dutch town, where I had the run of my guardian's wild acres and his great cool brick house. And then I went to college, began spending my vacations in New York or Europe . . ." He smiled at Dan, said, "I hope you'll come and see me—as well as Jill —whenever you have the opportunity," and added, "but I won't be selfish and keep you any longer. Jill, take your 'follower' and clear out."

So the moonlight was not wasted, after all. They collided with H. Chester on the veranda and Jill made the introductions briefly. When they'd gone on, Mr. Arden stood looking after them with an unreadable expression. Then he went into the house to see if his employer required anything more of him before he retired to his room.

"Let's go down in the rose garden," suggested Jill, "it's gorgeous, and the cutting beds around it are even lovelier by night, as they've planted so much white."

Dan said, "I stay away from rose gardens in moonlight. I know when I'm well off. How about sitting here?"

He had selected a rounding portion of the porch, clearly visible to anyone coming along, and dragged forth two big chairs almost to the rail. Jill settled herself in one with a cross between a sigh and a laugh. She didn't know another living man, she decided, who wouldn't have welcomed the opportunities of the rose garden. But you never knew what Dan would do.

"Your new boss is a very swell person," Dan said reflectively. "Mind if I smoke my pipe?"

"No, of course not. Yes, he's grand," she said.

"Funny, the name didn't convey a thing to me. Of course it's not uncommon. I remember hearing my dad talk about Charles Dennis. He was just a little tyke when he went fishing with him and my uncle Dick. But he remembered him well enough, and of course the older members of his family kept his memory green. They used to tell all sorts of stories about the kid from New York who came up to stay with his guardian and made a lot of friends. 'You'd never think he had a red cent,' my dad used to say, 'no sirree.'"

"Poor boy," said Jill, thinking of the young Charlie Dennis, farmed out among relatives. "Aunts and uncles and such, I suppose. Some of them tried to make a match between him and Mrs. Emory, when they were both kids, but it didn't come off. I dare say she's always regretted it. How's the job?"

"It's mostly walking around with a piece of string," he said solemnly, "and having conferences and looking at maps and blueprints and things. I found a funny old farmhouse to stay in. Nice. Lots of air and space. Plenty of flies, as they don't believe in screens, but the food is fine and the bed, if hard, is good for me, as far as that goes. I've no complaint. And you're near."

Jill waited. He asked briskly:

"Getting along all right?"

"So far."

"Who was the four-eyed gentleman we bunked into? He didn't look especially amiable, the little I saw of him."

"That's H. Chester. I've discovered what the H stands for. It's Heronimus."

"No foolin'?"

"No foolin'. When I told Jimmy he almost passed out."

"So you've been seeing Jimmy?"

"He came for a weekend. They all took quite a fancy to him. It's sweet of them," she said energetically, "to let me have my friends here, quite as if it were my house. I've a feeling, however, that neither Sally nor Elise approves of it . . . Although now that Jimmy has made such a hit they may think that the hired help has its uses."

"I'll start calling you Adversity."

"What?"

123

" 'Sweet are the uses—' " he murmured. "Look here, Jill, you want to keep your head in this job."

"I usually keep it on any job," she said indignantly.

"Quite. Perhaps I didn't mean your head. Perhaps I meant, hold on to your character. I'm tickled to death you've got such a nice one—job, not character, although that's all right too—and that you're with decent, substantial people, with more than a chance of staying with them for some little time to come. But your position's a little difficult as I see it."

"Dan Hardy, are you trying to tell me to keep in my place!"

"Not exactly. But you are employed here, to do certain things. You aren't an old friend of the girls, for instance, or of the family, who slipped naturally into a paid post without changing her status. On the other hand, Dennis seems to be the kind of man who won't have people around him who can't consider his home theirs. Nice attitude, might be mistaken sometimes," said Dan, "from what I know of people. You'll have to walk on eggs. If you were older it would all be comparatively easy, but you aren't much older than the kids you're here to look out after . . . certainly not older than the niece, what's her name? You have to steer a pretty middle course, seems to me. And another thing, don't let yourself be seduced by all this easy living." He broke off, laughed, knocked out his pipe against the rail. "There I go," he said ruefully, "lecturing again."

She said, ruffled:

"I'll manage all right. Don't worry about me."

"I wish you'd worry a little more about yourself," he told her.

She said, "Dan, you might tell me you're glad to see me!"

"Oh, woman!" said Dan, and sighed. "I refuse to commit myself to anything at this stage of the game. Perhaps someday I'll be in a position to tell you how glad—with demonstrations and gestures." He rose. "I've got to trek along back," he told her. "Early to bed and early to rise, that's how the Alger boys get along."

She went down on the lawns with him, and walked along the road to the gate. There he smiled at her, touched her shoulder lightly. "Good night," he said, "and remember all Uncle Dan told you."

"Bedtime story," she scoffed.

"Perhaps. See you later."

He had gone swinging off down the road. Jill returned to the house slowly. She had a feeling that H. Chester might be lying in wait for her, so she slipped up the stairs and to her own room, looking in on Mary before closing her door. Sally was still up, giggling across the corridor with her guest, a pert dark child with more manner than manners. Jill looked at her watch and then went out again and knocked at Sally's door.

They were both sitting cross-legged on the beds, and the air smelled of smoke. Jill said, "I wouldn't smoke in the bed if I were you, girls; lots of accidents have happened that way."

Sally made a face at her. Jill understood Sally's viewpoint perfectly. At seventeen Sally thought herself quite old enough to smoke. But her grandfather disapproved and had exacted a promise from her that she wouldn't, not for at least another year. It was hard on her, reflected Jill, all her friends smoked whether or not it was wise at their age. But Jill respected promises.

"I suppose you'll tell Grandfather," said Sally.

"No," denied Jill, "I won't. I'm not a tattletale. But you promised him, Sally, and you haven't very long to wait. I mean, I think you should either tell him outright that you're smoking, and then do it openly, or keep your word."

The little guest, Rosemary Hill, sniffed. She said, her snub nose in the air, "My mother doesn't care *what* I do! I think your grandfather's hopelessly old-fashioned, Sally."

Jill said, "You'd both better turn in, hadn't you? You've a date to ride with the Gaston boys and their sister before breakfast and to swim if there's time. You'll never wake up for it. Mary's sound asleep and I'm nearly so. 'Bye—"

She smiled at them, and went out. She hadn't closed the door tightly, and going down to her own room she heard Rosemary plainly, her clear young voice following her:

"I don't care, Sally, I think she's darned attractive!"

Jill stopped, as who would not. She was young and she was human.

She did not hear Sally's reply, but presently Rosemary asked:

"But what on earth does she do? Seems funny having a governess, or whatever she is, at your age."

Sally said scornfully, "She isn't a governess. She's a sort of—social snooper. Mary's crazy about her; personally, I think Gramp's the crazy one. Everyone's talking about her and laughing. As if I were feeble-minded or something and had to have a keeper!"

Jill's cheeks flamed and she found the sanctuary of her own room as quickly as possible. The old adage was true, she wished she hadn't listened. Sally was a brat and Jill despaired of ever winning her friendship.

She undressed and betook herself to bed with a book. But it did not hold her interest. She tossed it aside and lay back against the heaped pillows, her arms behind her head. She had a lot to think about: . . . Dan, living so near; Jimmy, given 'the freedom of the house; H. Chester and his unpleasant little ways. Presently she yawned and snapped out her light. If she had to get up and ride with those riotous kids in the morning at the ungodly hour of six o'clock she'd better catch a little shut-eye herself, she thought drowsily.

About an hour later she was awakened from her first deep sleep by a knock on her door. At first she thought she had dreamed it and sat up in bed, shaking the sleep from her eyes, listening. It came again, soft and persistent. It might be Mary, perhaps she felt badly, perhaps her cold was more severe than she'd fancied at first.

She called, "Is that you, Mary?" and waited. No answer came and she realized that, as Mary's room communicated with her own through a small passageway lined with cedar closets, it could not be Mary. She groped for her slippers and robe and then sat on the edge of her bed waiting. Presently she heard slow and cautious footsteps going off down the corridor.

She got back in bed again, shaking with anger. If it were H. Chester! That was, she thought furiously, a little excessive.

In the morning, returning from her ride with the young people, she climbed into her bathing suit and swam with them before breakfast, to which meal she, as well as they, brought an enormous appetite. It had been laid on a big table on the lawn under the maples, and Mr. Dennis presided cheerfully, delighted to have his chattering young guests. A blue jay screamed from a near-by tree and the air was warm and buoyant and salty. Elise had not made her appearance yet, Mary was staying in bed for at least part of the day, and H. Chester came down the dappled path of sunlight after they'd all finished.

Jill saw the Gastons off for home, went down to the bathhouses to pick up the wet and scattered towels. On her way back to the house to sit with Mary, she met H. Chester strolling toward her, a book under his arm.

She thought, There's no way out, I'll have to face him down with this, once and for all. I thought I could play along with him, keep off the thin ice. But I can't let him get away with a thing like that!

She asked abruptly, "Look here, Chester, did you knock at my door last night?"

"Of course not," he said, his eyes alert behind the glasses, "whatever made you think so?"

"Someone did," she stated, "quite a while after midnight. Everyone had gone to bed by then. I found that out by a little careful questioning this morning. Mary was asleep when I looked in at her at eleven, and

Sally and Rosemary's lights were out shortly thereafter. Mr. Dennis went to bed much earlier."

He said, smiling:

"Well, suppose for the sake of argument I did come
along to see if you were still up—you might be reading or something—you've told me yourself that you're
a night owl, what of it?"

"Plenty," she said angrily. "If you dare do anything
like that again, I'll go straight to Mr. Dennis. I don't
care what your motives were. Perhaps you wanted me
to heat you some milk, perhaps you needed a headache
tablet, perhaps you wanted to go walking in the dew
or discuss Shakespeare and musical glasses. Personally,
I don't care what you wanted. But if you ever come
sneaking around my door like that, I'll—"

He said, "I wasn't within a mile of your door, Jill,"
and she knew he lied. He looked, she thought, singu-
larly unpleasant for so inoffensive-appearing a young
man. "But if I happened to be I wouldn't advise you
to run to Mr. Dennis with a lot of trumped-up tales,"
he warned her, "as it's my word against yours. And
he's known me for a good bit longer than he has you."

All friendliness had departed. He was openly hostile.
Well, not long ago she had thought an armed truce
better than war, peace at whatever price her quick wits
were willing to pay. But now she had asked for war
and she had certainly got it, and no quarter given.

CHAPTER VIII

FOR the next few weeks life went along smoothly in the Dennis household. Dutifully Jill swam with the girls, rode with them, went with them to various daytime and evening parties, made things comfortable for the guests who came and went, held herself in readiness to make a fourth at contract or to play Sally's accompaniments when that young lady decided to sing; and now and then, at Mr. Dennis's urging, sang herself.

H. Chester, she believed, to her amazement, had learned his lesson. He gave her no trouble, was, perhaps, a little overcourteous, made no effort to be alone with her, and otherwise comported himself to her entire satisfaction.

Dan dropped over whenever he could. He did not force his advantage, refused dinner invitations more often than he accepted them, called for Jill several times in the car which had been given him for his own use while on the job, and sometimes strolled over of an evening to sit and talk with her. It was comforting to have him near, even if she did not see him a great deal.

Jimmy came down again, overnight this time in the middle of the week, and was promptly pre-empted by Elise for golf, and in the evening for a dance at the country club. As Mary was, and Mr. Dennis considered Sally, too young for these more adult festivities, neither was permitted to attend; therefore, Jill need not. Elise did not suggest her going and when Mr. Dennis asked, at dinner, "You're going, aren't you, Jill?" Elise spoke for her.

"No," Elise said, "she isn't, although I begged her on bended knee, practically. There'll be plenty of men to go around and a whirl would do her good."

Mr. Dennis looked pleased at this evidence of thoughtfulness, Jimmy startled, and Jill, for a moment, stunned. She caught Mary's knowing and indignant expression and Sally's slight, suppressed smile. Her own smile was radiant and her green eyes were as cool as winter skies.

"That's sweet," she said, "and perhaps—yes, I think I will change my mind!"

Elise's face was a study. Mary choked, apologized, hid her merriment in her dinner napkin. Sally shot a look at Jill, and for the first time her regard was admiring.

"That's fine," said Elise feebly.

Jill said briskly, "Perhaps I can get Dan . . ." She looked at Jimmy. "You remember Dan, don't you?" she asked maliciously.

Of them all, Mr. Dennis was wholly innocent. He commented "That will be nice, my dear," and turned to a vigorous carving of the family roast. H. Chester, sipping water as if it were rare wine, permitted himself a small, tight smile. He had never liked Elise and her discomfiture amused him, even though it had been brought about by Jill for whom he had unpleasant, if uncertain, plans.

After dinner Jill, humming carelessly, ambled to the telephone and called Dan at the farmhouse. She was gay and insistent.

"But you must," she insisted. "Of course, flannels and a blue coat. Now don't tell me you haven't them, Dan, because I know you have. You had 'em on the cruise and unless the moths . . . All right, we'll pick you up at ten."

While she was dressing Mary came in. She said, "Oh, Jill, you do look sweet!" And then she giggled. "Elise," reported Mary, "is fit to be tied!"

Jill paid no attention to her. She could not discuss Elise with the child and wild horses would not have made her admit to Mary what Mary knew as well as she, which was that Elise had not mentioned her going to the dance with them prior to dinner. "Like my dress?" she asked.

"Boy," said Mary, awed, "it's keen. When," she asked sighing, "can I adorn the body beautiful in something like that?"

"It won't be so long," prophesied Jill. "How are the scales holding up?"

"Fine," Mary told her. "Here, let me fix that shoulder strap. Ten and a half pounds," she reported, satisfied.

Jill settled the wide skirts of her best frock, the one she had not yet worn. It was cotton lace, simple, effective, white, with beautiful lines and exhibiting her slender waist to great advantage. Her burnished hair curling tightly over her little head, her green eyes shining, and her pretty mouth deeply reddened, she had never looked prettier and she knew it. When she ran downstairs with her wrap over her arm she found that Elise hadn't appeared as yet and Jimmy was playing billiards with Sally in the game room, while waiting.

They were having a good time. Sally was flushed and excited and Jimmy was laughing with her. Nice of Jimmy, reflected Jill, to be so pleasant to the younger girl. He looked up, saw her and put his cue in the rack.

"You look like sumpin'," he announced, "out of a book."

"Becky Sharp?" suggested H. Chester from the shadows, and Jill jumped. She had not seen him, as the light was concentrated over the billiard table.

"I hope that's a compliment, Chester," she said lightly. Sally was looking at her with more friendliness than usual. "That's a lovely dress," she said.

"I like it. I wish you were going," Jill told the girl sincerely.

"Isn't it absurd?" Sally asked, appealing to Jimmy. "Lots of girls my age go to these Wednesday night things. But just because there happens to be a little drinking and all that—mostly the young married crowd—" she added scornfully, "Grandfather won't hear of it. He keeps saying 'next year.'"

"It's a darned shame," agreed Jimmy, smiling at her. He went to Jill, put his arm through her own, walked off a step with her. He said, "You'll give Elise a lot of competition."

"With yourself?" she demanded. "Don't flatter yourself, Jimmy. I've other fish to fry."

Elise came in and after a time they trooped upstairs, Jill a little out of sorts. Somehow since this last visit of his she was growing irritated with Jimmy. What was it Chester had called her? An opportunist. Well, she wasn't, she told herself firmly, but Jimmy was . . .

135

ingratiating himself, making himself useful, playing up to Elise, the younger girls, and Mr. Dennis.

She felt responsible for Jimmy as she had introduced him into this household. Yet what could she say or do? There was nothing on which you could put your finger. He'd reply, if she taxed him, that it was through her he had met the Dennis family and if they liked him and accepted him what harm in that?

Jimmy drove the big car, sliding behind the wheel with satisfied ease. "Nice," he murmured, "to get your hands on a baby like this again . . ." and presently they stopped at the farmhouse for Dan. He climbed in back, after the greetings were over, with Jill.

"What's the big idea?" he murmured. "I'm not a dancing man . . . but there was a note in your voice—" He yawned frankly. "If it hadn't been there I wouldn't have come, I'm dead tired," he told her.

She said, "Hush. Be very attentive, will you? I'll tell you why later."

The club was a pleasant stone structure, the floor and orchestra excellent, the grounds ample, wooded, Japanese lanterns glowing in the trees, floodlights on the swimming pool, although the house committee hoped very much that the desire to swim would not seize certain impulsive and fully clothed young people as it had on previous evenings.

Dancing with Dan, Jill told him about the evening.

"She had no intention of asking me to go," she declared, "but of course she had to put her best foot forward with Uncle Charles. I was supposed to be a dear little girl and mutter that I wouldn't think of going, I had to study my algebra or something. Honestly, Dan, I couldn't let that challenge go by, you know I couldn't!"

"Of course not," he assured her, "but it won't make you any more popular with Mademoiselle Henshaw."

She shrugged. "I've given up hoping for anything from that quarter," she said.

"Jimmy seems to be doing all right."

"He makes me tired," said Jill vigorously; "he's slipped into this ménage as slick as a knife into butter: talks books with Mr. Dennis, plays tennis with Mary, is gallant to Sally, and devoted to Elise. Talk about an opportunist—and it's all my fault!"

"That," said Dan in admiration, "is a ten-cent word. Where'd you learn it?"

She looked at him reproachfully.

"I made it up," she replied; "ran it up on an old loom one day when Mr. Webster wasn't looking."

"Don't," Dan told her, swinging her across the floor and halting her at one of the French windows, "don't think too hardly of Jimmy. After all, he likes a bit of jam with his bread and butter."

They went out on the broad veranda, filled with

couples and groups of chattering people, and down on the lawn. Walking beside him, her face lifted to the cool breeze, she said:

"Well, he needn't procure his jam at the Dennises' expense. I don't like it at all."

He said gently, "That does you credit. You've noticed I keep away from too much obligation. But Jimmy makes hay while the sun shines. And so, my dear, do you."

She blazed at him, "That isn't so. I'm paid a salary. I work for it," she said.

"Is it such hard work?"

"No, of course not. That isn't the point. I do what I'm expected to do—and—"

He said, "And you've learned in the last few years to take what you can get and be thankful. So has Jimmy. There isn't much to choose between you."

She said angrily, "I wish I hadn't come. All you do is preach at me, Dan. You said yourself you were so glad I had a decent position with nice people."

He said, "But you don't in your heart look on it as a position. You regard it as an adventure which may last a year and may last six months. A stopgap."

Jimmy and Elise detached themselves from the shadows and came toward them. Jimmy said, "How about a turn, Jill?" and Elise smiled at Dan provocatively. He was personable enough, not that she cared for his type, but anything to teach Jill a lesson.

"I've been waiting for you to ask me to dance," she said.

"You've been forbiddingly popular," Dan told her.

Jill was silent as she and Jimmy danced. He asked:

"Cat got your tongue? Swell, isn't it? Had anything to eat? I was in the bar—how are the fish frying?"

"Jimmy, if you drink too much I'll never forgive you!"

"Who, me?" he demanded, injured. "Assume that I have a little sense, will you? Having a good time?"

"No," she said, "not particularly."

He said, unwilling to inquire the reason or uninterested, she didn't know which:

"Darn shame the old man won't let Sally come along. She's a grand kid—and she'd eat this up—right up her alley."

She said coolly:

"I hope you don't criticize Mr. Dennis's authority to Sally herself, Jimmy."

"What's come over you?" he demanded in amazement. "You aren't half the fun you used to be. Golly, if I had your opportunity! As to Sally, she's nearly eighteen."

"Not till late September."

"I know. She's asked me down to the party."

"I didn't know there was to be a party," said Jill.

"There will be. You're all returning to town right afterward, school opens the first week in October," said Jimmy calmly.

"It's a long way off," Jill told him, "and you—" She stopped as one of the older Gaston boys touched Jimmy's shoulder and cut in. He went on off the floor looking for Elise, and a little later Jill saw them dance by.

She found Dan, when the music stopped, out on the porch smoking. He said, as she came up, "How about it? It's my bedtime."

"You won't go to bed until the last dance is over," Jill said grimly, "if I know Jimmy or Elise, so you may as well stick it out."

She overslept the next morning and reached the dining room later than the others, and full of apologies. But Elise cut them short.

"Jill," she asked, and her manner was agitated, "did you notice me wearing my sapphire and diamond clip last night?"

Jill shook her head. She said, "I don't think so . . . yes . . . I do remember. I'm sure you had it on when you came down to the game room. You wore it on your shoulder, didn't you? I didn't notice it after that."

"Well, it's gone," said Elise flatly. "I was so tired last night I got out of my things any old way, thought

I'd left it on my frock, and when Jane was putting it away this morning I asked her to take it off. But it wasn't there."

"That's a shame," said Jill sincerely, and Elise pushed her coffee cup away and shook her head at scrambled eggs.

"I can't," she said. "I haven't any appetite. Uncle Charles, you remember the clip . . . Mother's stones, you had them reset for me at Christmas."

Her uncle said, "Yes, my dear. I suggest you telephone the club as soon as breakfast is over."

"I'll do it now," offered Jill, rising.

When she came back from the telephone her face was sober. "It hasn't been found," she told Elise; "they'll have men look for it today out on the grounds, you might have dropped it there."

Elise said, "I don't see how it was possible, the clasp was good."

"They're never good enough," Jill told her; "let's go down and look in the game room."

"It's not there, the room's been cleaned," said Elise, "and I've turned my room upside down and the halls have all been gone over. I'll be heartbroken," she said, "if it isn't found."

But it was not found that day, nor the next. Jimmy left, reluctantly, Elise taking him to the station. He was, reflected Jill, Elise's guest and not hers. Or so it seemed. She was playing croquet with Mary when the car drove in again and H. Chester, coming out of the house with some mail for the post office, hailed Elise.

"Wait a moment, will you?" he called. "I'll take the car back to the village, Mr. Dennis has some mail he wants to get out."

That reminded Jill of something. She stood with the mallet in her hand as Elise came toward them. She asked, "Did they take the cushions out of the car we were in the other night, Elise? I mean, to look for your clip?"

"With a fine-tooth comb," said Elise.

Chester, strolling up toward them, said maliciously: "Perhaps your clip's on its way to New York."

Elise looked at him, astonished, and Jill, her eyes widening, said coldly, "You'd better explain that, Chester."

He said, "Oh, it's nothing. I was thinking . . . Bates is, after all, a stranger to all of us—except to Jill."

Elise said heatedly, "Of all the absurd accusations. Have you lost your mind?"

Jill's hands were ice cold. She said, and her voice shook with rage:

"I think I'd better wire Jimmy's place, so that he can come back on the next train. He has a right to defend himself from a statement like that."

Mr. Arden blinked at her reproachfully through his

glasses, looking from one to the other of the girls, both with faces set against him, hostile and angry.

"Young Mr. Bates," he said placidly, "is fortunate in having two such attractive champions. I was joking, of course. I would as soon suspect the interesting Mr. Hardy—or yourself," he said slowly, with a funny, jerky little bow directed at Jill. He looked down at the letters in his hands. "Dear me," he said very like the White Rabbit, "I must hurry."

When he had driven off, Jill looked blankly at Elise. She asked:

"Do you suppose he meant that?" And Mary, an interested and silent spectator, whom they had all forgotten, burst out, "Of course he meant it, didn't you see his eyes?"

"I've never liked him," said Elise firmly. "As for poor Jimmy taking my clip!" She laughed. "It's too utterly absurd."

Jill said, "Isn't it? Jimmy's completely irresponsible of course and always hard up, but he would no more dream of doing a thing like that than I would." She frowned, tapping her mallet against her foot. "It's got to be found," she said furiously, "if every square inch of the club grounds has to be gone over."

Mary said, "Look, aren't we ever going to finish?"

Straightening up from her next shot, Jill became aware that Elise had not gone but was standing there, regarding her speculatively, with a very curious look in her eyes. She returned it steadily and after a moment Elise walked off. Jill reflected, overshooting the wicket when it came her turn, "Does she think for a minute . . . Oh, what's the matter with everybody, she thought disgustedly, permitting Mary to win the game with ease and speed in her distraction.

All that day she worried. It was silly but it was natural. If Arden thought that Jimmy . . . ? If Elise thought that she . . . ? It didn't make any difference that Jill was as convinced of Jimmy's innocence as of her own . . . the fact remained . . . the suspicion was ugly and threatening. That evening after dinner she knocked at Mr. Dennis's library door.

Arden was with him, and he was dictating to the younger man. "I'm sorry," said Jill, standing her ground, "but could I speak to you a moment alone, Mr. Dennis?"

"Why, of course," he told her, startled but courteous. He looked at Arden, murmured, "If you will excuse us for a moment . . ." and H. Chester departed, his back straight as a ramrod and as disapproving as a top sergeant's.

Jill said, "It's about Elise's clip."

"Has she found it?" asked Elise's uncle.

"No." She told him what Arden had said at the croquet ground. She added, "I don't think he meant it,

144

but I'm not sure. If he did, I feel that Jimmy should come back here and defend himself. It isn't fair to him not to ask him to come back. He is a stranger to you, of course," she said, trying to steady her voice, "and in a way I am too."

"My dear child!"

She said, "Oh, but you must consider it, and you don't know Dan Hardy either, he was with us, the other night. I expect him shortly, and I'd like the matter to be discussed in front of him." She flushed deeply but went on bravely, "And I'd like, too, to have my room and my personal belongings searched!"

He said, "Jill, my dear, you are taking this far too seriously. Such a ridiculous idea would never occur to me, or to any of us. Run along and forget it. I'll have a little talk with Chester. I can't believe for a moment that he would say such a thing except through a very mistaken sense of humor."

She said stubbornly, "I can't help it. I want my things searched. I won't feel easy until they are."

"Very well," said Mr. Dennis, "if it will relieve your mind at all. Suppose we have everyone in here."

Joseph knocked to say that Mr. Hardy was calling. "Ask him to come into the library," Mr. Dennis said. He turned to Jill. "Do you know Jimmy's telephone number?"

"Yes," Jill answered.

"Then get him," he said, "and ask him to return on the eight-o'clock train tomorrow." He had risen, he looked old and rather austere. "Such a thing has never happened under my roof," he said.

Jimmy, when she reached him, was querulous with astonishment. He cried, "Look here, what's up? I'm broke, I tell you, haven't a bean for train fare."

"Borrow it," said Jill, aware how her side of the conversation must sound to both Mr. Dennis and Dan, who had just come in, "and get here even if you have to walk. Something pretty serious has happened."

When she had hung up, Dan said:

"What's this all about, Jill?"

Mr. Dennis held up his hand to stop her hot rush of words. He explained:

"It's merely a misunderstanding. The night of the dance my niece lost a diamond and sapphire clip. It appears that my secretary had been ill-advised enough to suggest that someone under my roof—"

"I see," said Dan. He laughed, "Jimmy's all right, Mr. Dennis. I wouldn't take it as seriously as you are doing if I were you."

Jill said, "*I* take it seriously! Mr. Arden suggested further—oh, not exactly out and out—that if not Jimmy then you—or myself."

Dan's face stilled and hardened. He said, "I'd like

146

very well to have a quiet little talk with Mr. Arden—outside."

Meantime the others were on their way to the library: Elise, Arden, Mary and Sally. The servants, Mr. Dennis said, were out of the question . . . as out of the question, he had added, as Jimmy or Jill herself. "But," he said, "they are apt to be a little more sensitive, so we will leave them out of this if you don't mind."

When everyone was there, and the doors shut, Mr. Dennis turned to his secretary. He said mildly:

"Chester, Jill has told us that you have made a certain oblique accusation against Jimmy Bates, herself, and Mr. Hardy here concerning the matter of Elise's recent loss. I have no reason to doubt Jill's word; you did make the accusation, I am sure. But whether it was in jest or in earnest . . ."

Arden said, while Sally exclaimed, and Mary said loudly, "I heard him say it, grandfather," and Elise, her fair brows drawn, looked from one to the other.

"I did say something, Mr. Dennis, which might have been construed as an accusation. It was, however, I assure you, meant in a spirit of fun."

"I don't like that kind of fun," said Jill.

Arden shrugged. "I stated what was merely the truth . . . that neither Bates nor Hardy is very well known to the family and, after them," he bowed again in that jerky little way, "Jill herself."

Dan said, "After this is over I wonder if you'd like to stroll with me in the moonlight, Arden?"

Mr. Dennis said:

"Never mind that now. I am placed in an exceedingly difficult and painful position, but I understand Jill's feeling completely. Things like this do not lend themselves to jest, Chester. Jimmy is returning here tomorrow morning and Jill has demanded as her right that her room be searched."

Chester shrugged. He said, "Believe me, Mr. Dennis, this is all most distasteful to me, I had not meant to precipitate anything. But suppose at this juncture I remind you that such a search as Jill suggests would be merest farce, supposing for an instant that she had anything to conceal, as some time has elapsed since the loss of the clip."

Jill cried, "That settles it! We'll search the room now. And perhaps I will be able to prove to Mr. Arden's satisfaction that I haven't mailed a package of any kind since I've been here." She turned on her heel, and looked directly at Elise. "If you and Sally and Mary would come upstairs with me?"

Mary was almost in tears at this point and Elise and Sally both exhibited embarrassment. Elise said, "Jill, I assure you I don't want to—" and stopped, flushing.

That, thought Jill, is decent of her, she doesn't like me and never will, but she's fair. Sally too.

She said shortly:

"Come along."

When they were in her room they stood looking at her, not knowing where to begin. Jill, flinging herself in a chair, folded her hands. She said, "All right, get going, closets, handbags, suitcases, trunk, bureau drawers, everything. Don't overlook the tooth paste. I've read books about diamonds in tooth paste. When you're through I'll get out of this chair, you can pull out the cushions. . ."

Startled, they obeyed her automatically, tossing clothes out of the drawers, running their hands between mattress and bedspring, looking into pockets and boxes. Jill sat there, her face set in hard lines, and watched them. She was angrier than she had ever been in her life.

It was Mary who picked up the leather stamp box from the desk, shook it idly, opened it and turned, perfectly white, to the others, an exclamation dying on her lips, and the clip in her hand.

CHAPTER IX

MARY said stupidly:

"But—here's the clip."

Jill sat perfectly still in her chair. She could not have moved if her life had depended on it. Sally cried, bewildered, "Mary!" and went over and took the clip in her own hand as if she could not believe the evidence of her eyes and must resort to her sense of touch. Elise exclaimed, *"Well!"* on a rising note, and Jill found herself, after all, getting to her feet.

She said flatly, "I don't believe it!"

She was whiter than Mary and her eyes were so dark that no one could have told their color. She said, without looking again at the clip, without touching it:

"I didn't take it. I haven't anything more to say, Elise."

Elise said slowly, "I believed you before, Jill." She looked the other girl up and down and said coolly, "I never liked you—but I couldn't believe you were a thief."

Mary rushed over to Jill, and put her arms about her.

"She isn't," she said, crying again, "don't you dare say that, Elise Henshaw, she isn't!"

"How does she explain the clip's being in the stamp box?" demanded Elise coolly, as if Jill were not present.

"I don't explain it," said Jill, "because I don't know how it got there. I have a pretty good idea . . . but no proof." She broke away from Mary's hard, loyal clasp and before Sally could prevent her, snatched the clip from her hand. The door slammed behind her and the three girls looked at one another in astonishment.

Elise said, half hysterically, "She can't get away with that!"

"Don't be a goof," said Mary, sniffling, "she's going downstairs to Grandfather!"

Sally shrugged her slender shoulders. She said, "I hate scenes . . . I'm going to my own room."

Elise, following her, was halfway out of the door when she turned. She said sharply, "Do stop crying, Mary, you'd think the world had come to an end just because that girl turned out to be what you might have expected in the first place."

Mary said, still sobbing:

"You make me sick! You like her friends well enough . . . suppose your darling Jimmy put the clip

151

in the box! Oh, don't glare at me. You've been crazy about him ever since he first came to the house. You've been trying to get him away from Jill."

Sally had stopped to listen. Elise said in disgust:

"You needn't inform the entire household, Mary. And I didn't know that there was any 'getting away,' as you so prettily phrase it. Jimmy and Jill have been friends for some time, there's nothing whatever between them, and I happen to know it. He could have been as mistaken in her as we were."

"We were not," said Mary, stamping her foot. "At least I wasn't."

Sally put her arm around the younger girl and drew her out into the hall. "Come along with me," she said quietly.

Mary stared at her. She said, "You don't believe it, do you, Sally?"

"No," said Sally, "I don't. I don't know why, but I don't."

The three men left in the library started up when the door flew open. Dan and Mr. Dennis had been making small talk, avoiding all unpleasant subjects, and Arden said nothing, sitting back in his usual corner, in the big leather chair, with the reading light behind him. When the door opened they looked up and saw Jill standing there. She was so white that she was ghastly and her disheveled curls were flung back from her face. She walked in, and laid the clip on the desk, and Dan's breath whistled in his throat and Mr. Dennis made a small hurt sound. Only Arden, watching, made no sound.

"Here is the clip, Mr. Dennis," Jill said, trying to keep her voice steady. "Mary found it. Among my things. I didn't steal it. I did not know it was there. It was put there by someone who— But that doesn't matter. I haven't an atom of proof."

"My dear Jill!" said Mr. Dennis, bitterly distressed and looking from her to Dan.

Dan walked over and stood close to her, not touching her but very near. He asked:

"What's the next move, Jill?"

"If you'd wait for me?" she asked him. "I'll put some things in a bag. Perhaps your landlady would keep me for the night? Jimmy will be down in the morning. I'll wait for him, and we can go back together to town." She turned and looked at Mr. Dennis. She said, and for the first time her voice broke, "I'm so grateful to you—for all you've done. I—I'll leave my last month's salary . . . I hadn't spent it or sent it to the bank. And the clothes. I'll have to take a suitcase and just a few things. I'll pay you back, Mr. Dennis."

He said, "Jill, wait a minute. It's an unfortunate misunderstanding. There must be some explanation."

Arden's face was clear and hostile in the circle of light. He stared at Jill steadily, saying no word, and she stared back. She said, "There is, of course, but I don't know it. Or can't give it." She put her hand on Dan's arm and said piteously, as if it had just occurred to her, "I—now that you have the clip again you wouldn't have me arrested, would you?"

"Jill," said Mr. Dennis, "I don't understand this at all. I can't believe . . . I *won't* believe . . . and yet . . . Mary found it, you say, among your things? Could not Elise have dropped it in your room the night of the dance?"

"She wasn't in my room that night," Jill told him, "and if she had been she wouldn't be likely to drop it in a leather stamp box and put it in the desk drawer. And if a maid had happened to find it she wouldn't have done that either, she would have known to whom it belonged."

She paused a moment and as Elise came in the room she heard herself say as if she were very tired, "I'm sorry, Mr. Dennis."

She passed Elise as if she did not see her, and Dan followed. He called, "I'll wait down here for you, Jill," and then stood a moment in the door to inquire, "May I use your telephone, to get a taxi from the station? It's too far for her to walk—she's pretty upset."

Mr. Dennis said in agitation, "My boy, I assure you

I can't believe . . ." He put his hand in bewilderment to his forehead. "But—I can't keep her here, if she insists. I'm sure this will be cleared up. See if you can't persuade her to come back here tomorrow."

"If you think I'll stay in the house with her!" said Elise suddenly.

Arden spoke for the first time.

"It is all very distressing," he said precisely. "I am grieved that a chance remark of mine should have brought it about. Perhaps, however, it is just as well."

"Will you kindly keep your mouth shut!" said Dan savagely.

He went to the telephone under the stairs and called the station taxi rank. Mr. Dennis came out to him as he sat there, looking taller than ever and very stooped. He said, "There's no necessity . . . I'll have one of the cars . . ."

"Thanks," said Dan and tried to smile, "but we'll manage."

A little later Jill extricated herself from Mary's damp, violent embrace and came down. Sally had walked with her to the head of the stairs. She said thoughtfully, "There's something very fishy about this, Jill. I'm awfully sorry." She regarded Jill with clear blue eyes. "I haven't been especially nice to you," she said, and looked suddenly no older than Mary, "but

155

Elise—she's a dreadful cat—put me off. I really liked you all along. But I was jealous of you."

Out of her own tumult of pain and rage and terror Jill found a moment in which to smile and ask quite naturally, "Why?"

"Oh," said Sally, "you're awfully attractive—Rosemary thought so too—and you've had such an exciting life. You're free," said Sally, not quite eighteen and feeling tremendously imprisoned.

Jill touched her shoulder.

"Not very," she said briefly. "Good-bye, Sally."

Dan came up the stairs to meet her and took the suitcase. "Taxi coming right up," he said. A horn tooted in the driveway. "There it is. Jill, are you wise leaving like this? It isn't like you. Why don't you face it out? I don't believe a soul here believes seriously—"

"I don't care what they believe," she said furiously, "and I don't care if you do think I'm running away. I am." She lifted her little chin high and added, "I'll get along, I have before. I will again. But . . . I keep thinking . . . Perhaps I'll never get another job, with this against me? I can't ask for—for references. And there's Mrs. Emory. She'll be so unhappy . . . she's been so kind to me."

In the cab she leaned her forehead against his shoulder and cried. He put his arm about her, held her there, offered a large clean handkerchief, but made no attempt to quiet her. She'll be better off, he thought, for a good cry.

His landlady, spare and forbidding, was a little perturbed when confronted with a pretty, redheaded girl whose eyelids were pink and whose nose was pinker. A redheaded girl with green eyes who was, very obviously, in trouble of some sort. But Mrs. Giffin liked Dan. During the little while he had been with her she had grown fond of him. So when he asked, "Could you put up Miss Hamilton for the night, Mrs. Giffin? She's returning to New York in the morning, I think," Mrs. Giffin replied, "Well, if you say so, Mr. Hardy."

She went upstairs with Jill, ushered her into a small, cheerful back room. "Bathroom's two doors down," she announced. "Mr. Hardy's across the hall. I'm next door," she added with a sharp look. "I hope you'll be comfortable. I suppose you've had your supper," she added at the door, "but if you'd like a glass of milk or a doughnut . . ."

"Yes, I've had supper," said Jill, a little hysterically.

"Aren't you the young lady over to the Dennise's?" asked Mrs. Giffin, lingering.

"Yes," said Jill shortly. "Please, Mrs. Giffin, may I speak to Mr. Hardy for a minute?"

"He's coming up with your suitcase," announced Mrs. Giffin. "I don't see any harm in talking," she went on significantly, and stood back to let Dan enter.

"Put the suitcase on the chair," said Jill. She opened it, exhibited garments thrown in helter-skelter, at random. Toilet articles, a bankbook, and something else, wrapped in a handkerchief. She said, "I did steal something, after all."

Mrs. Giffin luckily was out of earshot, but she had left the door open. Dan said, horrified, "You did what!"

"The stamp box, there in the handkerchief. No, don't touch it. There are marks on it. Fingerprints . . . that is, I think they are . . . dark, oily . . . They weren't there before. It always stood on the desk, it is a pretty little box, I noticed it each time I sat down to write. I didn't keep stamps in it, I bought books and put them in the drawer. Someone opened it to put the clip in there."

"Mary opened it when she found it, didn't she?" asked Dan.

"Yes, of course. She flipped back the lid, it's hinged, and there was the clip. She took it out, she didn't touch the box again. Even if her prints were on it, the others will show too. You didn't think for a moment I was going to let anyone get away with that? I've a friend on the force," Jill added, and at another time Dan would have laughed, she spoke so portentously, "he'll tell me what to do. Fingerprint people and all that. And I'll make every living person in that house consent to be printed . . . or know the reason why."

"Jill, you read too many mysteries. Look, do you suspect anyone definitely?"

"Chester Arden, of course."

"But why?"

She said wearily, "Call it my fatal beauty, or anything you want. He was very friendly until . . . until he discovered that I wasn't going to be."

"Why, the little—!"

"Yes," she said hastily. "But oh, Dan, for goodness' sake, stop swearing. Mrs. Giffin will hear you and put us both out. And I'm tired enough to drop. Will you do something for me?"

"Of course."

"In the morning, can you get away without losing your job? I'm not going back to New York till I see Jimmy. Will you go over there with me? No, to the station first. He's taking the eight-o'clock down."

"Okay. Look, honey, you try and get some sleep."

She went up to him, put her hand on his arm. "Dan," she said anxiously, "you don't believe—?"

He said, "I wouldn't believe it if I saw it with my own eyes, Jill!"

"Thanks," she said and tried to smile, "you're sweet. Now go away before I start crying again, for I'm feeling pretty sorry for myself."

"Wait a minute," Dan said, "I'm going to send Mrs. Giffin up with a cup of hot milk for you. Mind you drink it."

He went off and she heard him calling his landlady. Jill sat down on the edge of the sagging mattress, too tired to undress and wondering whether in her frantic packing she had included a nightgown. Absurdly the thought of nightgowns was the last straw—all her lovely clothes, which she had accepted with such utter nonchalance . . . They could hang there in the Dennis closets till they rotted, she thought, and the tears rolled down her tired face and she put her red head in her hands and wept like a forlorn child. Why— why had she placed herself in a position where people could do these things to her? If she'd handled Arden properly; or if she hadn't tried to handle him at all, if she'd relied on Mr. Dennis's sense of justice and had gone to him in the beginning?

Mrs. Giffin came in, carrying a cup and saucer. She said, "You poor child," and sat down on the bed beside Jill. The cup rocked in her hand, she set it down on a small table and put her spare arms about her guest. She said, "I don't know what it's all about, but Mr. Hardy says you've run into stormy weather. There. Don't cry any more. Let me get you to bed. The milk's boiling. It will cool and then you can drink it."

Jill submitted gratefully and when presently in the

nightgown which Mrs. Giffin had discovered, after all, she lay back against the hard but comforting pillows, Mrs. Giffin brought the cup to her.

"It's bitter," said Jill, rousing.

"Something to make you sleep," said Mrs. Giffin. "Mr. G, he was a great sufferer. Couldn't sleep no more than one—two hours a night. These pills helped. Doctor gave them to him, perfectly harmless, just relaxes your nerves. Mr. Hardy said they'd be good for you. I'm going to put out the light and open the window and sit here a little till you go to sleep. Try not to cry any more. I know how you feel," she ended sympathetically. "I suffered a great loss . . . when Mr. G died."

Jill was a little dazed. What had Dan told the woman? Dan, down in the kitchen, his eyes grave, had said, "I wouldn't press her too closely about things, Mrs. Giffin . . . she's had a great shock . . . a loss, you know," he said vaguely.

Jill slept and dreamed that Mrs. Giffin had lost a diamond clip and that Elise was wringing her hands over the coffin of someone who was obviously Mr. G but who looked very like Axel, the fire-eater, with whom Jill had become well acquainted in her short Coney Island experience, and that Arden, H. Chester himself, was the Cheshire Cat, grinning at her from the branches of an enormous tree, his bewhiskered face

161

receding and advancing and his thin voice stating, very catlike, *I told you so—*

She woke and lay still a moment trying to reconcile herself to her strange surroundings. A low-ceilinged room, bird's-eye maple, a washstand, the pitcher riotous with red flowers, tatting edging the cover on the bureau and a faded patterned wallpaper, little blue roses in flowerpots.

Suddenly she remembered and sat up. The house seemed still and the sunlight was very bright, brighter than it should be so early in the morning.

Jill groped under her pillow for the inexpensive, accurate watch she had carried for five years and, looking at its face, could not believe her eyes. She shook it and held it to her ears. Yes, the watch was going. And it said thirty minutes past ten.

"Mrs. Giffin!" shouted Jill at the top of her lungs.

Footsteps hurrying down the hall rewarded her. Mrs. Giffin opened the door and put her graying head inside. "Awake, dearie?" she inquired unnecessarily.

"Yes. Is it really ten-thirty? Oh, for Pete's sake, what happened?" demanded Jill distracted, her hair wild all over her head and her little face pink from sleep. "Where's Dan . . . ? We were to meet Jimmy at the station."

"There," said Mrs. Giffin, "it's all right. You had a good sleep and that's what we wanted for you. Mr.

Hardy left word you weren't to worry, he'd meet your friend, and he'd come back here afterwards. You were sleeping like a baby when I came in this morning to get the little box out of the suitcase."

"The little box!" cried Jill.

She jumped out of bed and ran in her bare feet to the suitcase. The stamp box was gone. "But, why on earth—" she began.

"Mr. Hardy said it was something you wanted to return," said Mrs. Griffin. "Aren't you hungry?"

"Hungry?" repeated Jill wonderingly, as if she had never heard the word. "I'm starved!"

"That's fine," said Mrs. Giffin. "I'll have something ready when you come down. How do you want your eggs?"

Jill bathed and dressed, her mind with Dan. What on earth did he mean, acting in so highhanded a fashion—running off with her stamp box, going alone to meet Jimmy—drugging her last night! Drug was the word, she told herself melodramatically.

The dress in which she had left the Dennis house was not wholly suitable for morning wear, but she put it on, not having any other, as even the old clothes she thought of as her own were in the trunk at the Dennis house—and went down to the cheerful sunny kitchen where eggs were frying in a spider and the smell of coffee was potent and heartening. Her head felt a little heavy and her eyes, but she was rested through and through and sitting there, looking on the patch of bright flowers beyond the window, she wondered why she had run away. She hadn't meant to; it wasn't because she was so frightened, it was because she had been so utterly bewildered. She would have stayed, faced them, accused Arden outright, no matter how like malice and a vain effort at self-defense it would have sounded.

The big gray tomcat purred near the stove, he had a pleasant expression even when he fell suddenly asleep. If she ever had a home of her own, thought Jill, she'd have a cat. Any room was more comfortable with a cat in it.

She had just finished her breakfast and was beginning to think that she should be a lot angrier with Dan than she was when she heard a car stop outside and a moment later his voice. She jumped up from the table and ran out to the front door and down the steps, and then stood stock still. Dan and Jimmy—and Mr. Dennis.

Her knees gave way, for no good reason, and she sat down suddenly and smartly on the steps. Mr. Dennis hurried toward her.

"Jill, my dear," he said, "if you could forgive us all out of the generosity of your heart . . ."

She asked, looking from one to the other:

"Chester did put the clip in my room?"

"Yes," said Mr. Dennis and looked old and sad, "he did."

"But why—" began Jill.

She didn't mean, Why did he do it? She knew why he had. Mr. Dennis said, "Perhaps you can tell us why, Jill, if you wish. Or perhaps you'd rather not. But I think we know."

Jimmy was making silly faces at her. She hadn't spoken to either him or Dan. She asked, "But how did you find out?"

Dan said, "Jimmy. That is to say, Jimmy saw him pick up the clip from the game room floor the night of the dance."

"Why, Jimmy Bates!" Jill jumped to her feet. "Why didn't you say something about it?"

"Never occurred to me," said Jimmy, grinning. "Saw him pick up something sort of shiny, couldn't tell what it was, and put it in his pocket. Never gave it another thought till Dan met me this morning. Then it popped back into the old mind. *Must* have been the clip. But it was dark over in that corner where he was. Elise stood there a moment before we went out, you know, then she went on ahead of us to leave an order or something. Met us upstairs in the hall. Remember? Of course he could have picked up anything else. I mean, I hadn't any proof. But Dan and I decided coming

165

along to the house that I'd bluff it and see what happened. And the stamp box clinched things."

"How?" demanded Jill.

"There were prints on it. You're a smart child," said Jimmy with approval, "they were marks made by a dirty hand. Ink or oil. After dinner sometime Arden changed a ribbon on his typewriter—he came down to the game room apparently with every idea of washing his hands in the lavatory there. Then he took to watching the game for a bit. And Elise lost her pin. That gave him his bright idea for his good deed for the week. He forgot all about his hands."

Mr. Dennis said, "Jill, you'll come back to us . . ."

She said, "Of course. I'm sorry I ran away . . . it was a stupid thing to do. I knew who'd hidden the clip in the stamp box, but I couldn't prove it and I thought, if I could get away and think things through—"

Dan murmured, "Chester has got away and is thinking things through."

He glanced at Mr. Dennis who looked, for a man of years and dignity, remarkably guilty. Jimmy said delightedly:

"He went off in his own car. But Mr. Dennis sent a man to drive him. Poor Heronimus!"

"Poor who?" exclaimed Mr. Dennis.

"Heronimus Chester Arden," said Jimmy solemnly, "was in no condition to drive. Dan took him down past the tennis courts, back of the garage, and talked to him like a couple of Dutch uncles."

"You didn't!" cried Jill, delighted.

Dan looked at his knuckles. He said, "I did. He had it coming to him, on several counts. Mr. Dennis preferred to have him go quietly, we none of us wanted any publicity. So I undertook to see that he went quietly. He's a very queer egg indeed. He didn't put up a fight—I don't mean with me . . . I mean when Jimmy said calmly, 'But I saw you pick up Miss Henshaw's clip, Arden,' he went all to pieces, and when we produced the stamp box—"

"Come," said Jimmy. "Don't stand there looking all starry-eyed with wonder, Jill. Let's get back to the house. The girls want to go swimming and they won't stir without you. And personally I'm tired both of talking and of refereeing . . . and I've work to do."

"Work!" repeated Jill, and looked from one to the other. Mr. Dennis smiled, Dan's face was unreadable, and Jimmy grinned impishly.

"Well," he said, "one nail drives out another, doesn't it? Arden's gone the way of all flesh and—"

"And what?" said Jill impatiently. "You do talk in riddles, Jimmy!"

"And," said Jimmy, "P.S. . . . I got the job!"

CHAPTER X

"Why, Jimmy Bates!" exclaimed Jill, astonished, incredulous.

Mr. Dennis proffered the explanations. It had occurred to him, he said, that Jimmy might be willing to help him out for a few months. He could use a typewriter, he could take dictation, employing a sort of unique shorthand of his own, he was book-minded; and he had an authentic interest in literature.

It dawned upon Jill suddenly that Mr. Dennis had not become aware of these qualifications in the twinkling of an eye, or rather in the twinkling of Dan's hard fist. Jimmy must have prepared the soil for just this on his previous encounters with the older man. Mr. Dennis went on mildly:

"It isn't of course the sort of thing that Jimmy wants to do—permanently—but he has been kind enough to say that he'll fill in. He understands that the son of a very old friend of mine is at present in business college and when he finishes I intend to take him on. This arrangement was made several years ago. Chester—"

he made a wry face—"understood it also. So it isn't any more than a stopgap that I have to offer Jimmy but—"

"Suits me," said Jimmy, beaming. "Stop looking so aghast, Jill. How about a spot of congratulation?"

Mr. Dennis said somewhat anxiously:

"I thought it would please you, Jill."

Bless his unworldly heart, she thought, and felt the sting of tears in her eyes, he wants to make it all up to me and he thinks, what better way than to give my young man a job . . . She said, smiling:

"It does. It's grand." She held out her hand to Jimmy. She said solemnly, "And don't go foolin' round stamp boxes!"

So it ended in laughter. Only Dan did not seem moved to mirth. He left for work before Jill had a chance to be alone with him, but Mr. Dennis exacted his promise to appear at dinner that evening. And presently having bid farewell to her hostess, the good woman curious to the point of frenzy and utterly bewildered by the alteration in her overnight guest, Jill went back in the Dennis car.

It was something of a triumphant return. Mary was hopping impatiently about the drive, waiting for the car, and rushing out threw her arms around Jill's neck. "I knew it!" she cried, exultantly, "The nasty little beast— Would have served him right if Grandfather had put him in jail!"

169

Sally was less emotional, but when she took Jill's hand in her own and said, "I'm glad you're back," Jill was bound to believe her. And Elise, her poise deserting her for once, stumbled through a form of apology.

"I'm so sorry, Jill," she said. "It was incredibly stupid of me to believe for a moment. . . ."

Jill said, "Please don't give it another thought Elise. I would have thought the same in your place of course. Pretty strong circumstantial evidence, I'd say."

Jimmy, his hands in his pockets, regarded them all with the expression of the conscious god from the machine. He had worked this miracle and gloried in it. Jill might be the moment's heroine, but he was the hero. As yet the other three girls did not know of his altered standing. He told them now and was gratified by their immediate and articulate delight.

"Goody for our side," said Mary definitely, "you'll be lots of fun to have around, Jimmy." And Sally smiled at him, and Elise's pale and pointed face was briefly animated.

Mr. Dennis was sending the car to town on an errand, and it was arranged to have Jimmy's things picked up at his lodgings. Jill overheard him discussing it with Mr. Dennis—

"That is, if the old harridan will let them go. You see," explained Jimmy unabashed, "I owe a little rent."

Mr. Dennis evidently took a wallet from his pocket. Jill could not see, but she could hear him say:

"A little advance by way of reward? Will this be enough?"

"It sure will. Thanks a lot," said Jimmy cheerfully, "I'll pop it in an envelope with a note. I'm very much obliged to you, Mr. Dennis, you've been swell. Of course it was unthinkable that Jill—I mean anyone who really knew her wouldn't dream for an instant . . . I'm glad I happened to be around that night. That was my good luck. If I hadn't, I'm afraid I couldn't have done much convincing despite my convictions in the face of the evidence."

"Poor child," said Mr. Dennis, "I hope she'll forgive us."

"Sure," said Jimmy, "she's forgiven you already. Jill doesn't hold grudges. She's a grand girl—and she hasn't had a very easy time these last years," he ended soberly.

Jill walked away from the library windows. She was grateful beyond words that Jimmy had just happened to see Chester pick up the clip; and grateful, too, that he should speak of her to Mr. Dennis with loyalty and affection. But, she thought, he needn't be so darned patronizing about it! As if I were about six and with a little more brains could easily be a half-wit!

She was decidedly uneasy about Jimmy's careless

stepping into the household, his calm usurping of the place Chester had vacated. It was so—taking things for granted. So utterly Jimmyish. She spoke about it to Dan that night when, after a very pleasant, rather gay dinner, she went walking with him along the beach. Elise had drawn Jimmy into a game of contract with her uncle and an elderly gentleman who had dropped in for the evening. So Jill was free.

She said seriously:

"I hope to heaven Jimmy won't pull any boners. After all, I'm responsible for introducing him here."

"He hasn't the qualifications for the perfect male secretary," replied Dan, laughing, "he's not sufficiently negative, but he'll get along. I wouldn't worry if I were you."

"I wasn't thinking of secretarial qualifications," said Jill. She drew a deep breath and looked out over the sparkling water, the golden moon path which lay across the ripples. Far out a boat went by, her lights shining; and near-by boats lay at anchor, their riding lights like fallen stars.

Dan said:

"Jill, I had a letter today from a man in my old South American outfit. There's a chance I may go back."

She said, startled and disturbed, "How marvelous for you, Dan. It's what you want, isn't it?"

"Yes. Not South America especially. It wouldn't matter if it were Arizona, Kamchatka, Siberia, China. But anywhere where I'd have a good gang to boss, a hard job to do, and a blueprint to turn into a bridge or a railroad. Any place where I could get out and sweat, work with my hands, and come back to a shack or a tent at night, dog-tired but knowing that I'd advanced things a little." He paused. He said, after a moment, "I've never regretted going on from job to job. But this time it would be different. There'd be you."

She said, "That's sweet of you, Dan."

"Oh, don't say the expected things. You know how I feel. Well, maybe nothing will come of it. Listen, didn't someone call?"

It was Elise. They heard her voice again and came back across the lawns to the house. She stood in the doorway, the light behind her.

"Jill . . . ?"

"Coming," shouted Jill.

When they reached the steps Elise smiled down at them apologetically:

"Would you be angels and take Jimmy's and my place? I've just had a telephone from the Maynards. Some people motored down from Westchester this evening, an old school friend of mine among them, haven't seen her for years . . . Jimmy said he'd run me over. . . ."

Jill said, "Well, I've never played with Dan. He may be very bad."

"I'm rotten," confided Dan sincerely.

"I'm sure you're not," Elise told him absent-mindedly. "Thanks a lot."

Going in to join the bridge game Jill thought, Elise can drive herself nicely. If not, there's a chauffeur or two around. But naturally she'd take Jimmy!

As she was undressing that night, Sally knocked at her door.

"May I come in, Jill?"

"Do. Take a pew," offered Jill cordially. "What's on your mind, Sally?"

She looked at the younger girl and thought for the hundredth time how pretty she was. She was especially so now, the yellow hair tied back with an apple-green ribbon, her slender figure wrapped in a black and gold robe over apple-green pajamas. Sally, perching on the bed, hugged her knees in her arms and commented:

"Our dear cousin Elise is making a play for your boy friend, Jill."

Jill said crossly, "He isn't my boy friend, Sally."

Sally opened her cornflower eyes. "Isn't he? He told me he was."

"Drat him," said Jill, laughing in spite of herself, "he always did take too much for granted."

"Isn't he, really?"

174

"Well, it's this way," explained Jill briskly, creaming her face. "I've known Jimmy a long time. We've had a lot of fun together. I've been lonely a good deal, Sally, and sometimes when you're lonely you get frightened. . . . You wouldn't know about that," she mentioned, wiping the cream away and regarding her shining skin with satisfaction. She took off the net cap which protected her hair, picked up a brush, and began to brush in long even strokes.

Sally said, "You've the loveliest hair, Jill!"

"You should see me brush it in winter," Jill told her, "wild it is, all full of sparks. I feel like a witch."

"Go on about Jimmy," ordered the younger girl.

"There isn't much. Now and then he thought . . . or I thought . . . that perhaps we could be serious about each other. Rarely simultaneously, if you know what I mean. Didn't amount to a thing, Sally, even if either of us could have afforded to be serious."

"You wouldn't be happy," announced Sally serenely, "because you're too much alike."

Jill dropped the brush with a little clatter.

"Jimmy and I—alike?" she repeated. She thought, Oh dear, there must be some truth in it. Dan first, now Sally!

Sally said, "Yes, of course you are. In some ways. But he'd be a lot worse off with Elise," she said soberly. "Elise doesn't know how to play . . . not really.

Oh, she rushes around and screams a lot, you know, that sort of thing, but she isn't in the least mad really. Mad, I mean, in the nice way that Jimmy's mad."

"You know a lot about Jimmy," said Jill, smiling, and picked up the hairbrush again, "not having seen him very often."

"He isn't hard to know," said Sally. She jumped off the bed and to Jill's intense surprise came over and kissed her cheek. She said, "Good night. I'm so glad you're here. I expect I've been pretty brutal to you, haven't I? I didn't mean it. I do like you a lot—"

She departed, yellow hair, blue eyes, apple-green pajamas. Jill sat staring at the door long after it had shut. "I wonder what all that meant?" she inquired aloud. Then she shook her head and switched out the lights. It probably didn't mean a thing, she thought; I must be getting jumpy.

She was awakened about one o'clock by the sound of voices below her windows which overlooked the driveway. She recognized Elise's high clear laugh and heard Jimmy say, "Run along in, I'll put the car away."

"Don't talk so loud," said Elise, "you'll wake the dead."

Jill slipped out of bed and went to the windows, kneeling by the sill. She could see them dimly and hear them, although their voices were lowered now.

"Ouf!" said Elise. "I'm tired. Marvelous, wasn't it,

how they all fell for the school friend story?" She giggled.

"Hush," ordered Jimmy cautiously. He yawned prodigiously. He said, "Next time you take me dancing to the Golden Dove I'll wear hobnails so I can retaliate when stepped on."

They stood there a moment and Jill could have sworn that she saw Jimmy's arm go around Elise, that she saw him bend his head. But she had no proof . . . just two dark figures which for an instant drew close together. Then one shadow detached itself and went into the house and presently the car pulled out cautiously around the drive toward the garage.

Jill went back to bed. It wasn't any of her business if Jimmy and Elise went dancing at the Golden Dove— which was a fairly conspicuous roadhouse some twenty miles away—and it wasn't any of her business if they lingered in doorways. What Jimmy did after working hours was not her concern, nor was Elise her problem. But, as she had told Dan, she was responsible for Jimmy's coming here.

She spoke to Jimmy the first chance she had the following morning. She said directly:

"I heard you and Elise come home last night. And what you said. About dancing at the Golden Dove."

"You're a light sleeper," he said ruefully. "Won't give us away, will you?"

She said angrily, "It's nothing to me. But why do you have to go to such pains to deceive anyone. All that elaborate school friend business!"

"Elise's idea," said Jimmy calmly. "She was roped into the bridge game, and bored to death. Her uncle doesn't approve of the Golden Dove. You must see that, while he's a good soul, he's a bit on the outmoded side. As for me, I thought the school friend gag was bona fide, till we got away from the house."

"You're being very foolish," Jill warned him. "Mr. Dennis has given you a good job, a pleasant home, and not too much work. He won't like you planning things with Elise behind his back. Anyway, Jimmy, you're employed here, as much as I am . . . a flirtation with one of the members of the family isn't a good idea at all."

"Jealous, darling?"

"I am not," she said, "and you know it."

"I'm afraid I do. You don't go for me at all, do you, any more?" he asked sighing. "Elise is all right. Don't worry about me . . . I'm not getting myself into anything. She doesn't mean anything. She's bored that's all, and the old man keeps her on a tight rein," he added.

"That's because she—" Jill could have bitten her tongue off. She was not going to gossip with Jimmy about the Dennis family. Not any more.

"Because she what?"

"Oh, Mr. Dennis is a sort of guardian," said Jill vaguely.

"You didn't mean that. Elise is past the guardian age. You meant . . . because of the little scandal some years ago? Don't look so agape. I know all about it, she told me last time I was here. But don't be scared, Jill, I'm not jeopardizing my present berth for Elise. Besides," he added calmly, "she hasn't any money of her own."

"Jimmy Bates!"

He said, laughing, "Don't be so shocked. This catch-as-catch-can business isn't much good. About the best way to get money is to marry it." He grinned at her. "You wouldn't fill the bill, sweetheart. Elise won't. I'll just have to keep my eyes open."

She cried, "Jimmy, what's come over you? I think you're crazy. At least it's the kindest thing to believe."

He said, "I'm tired of this pillar-to-post business. You should be too. Face facts. Dan's out . . . he'll never make more than a mere living. I'm out . . . naturally —both ways. Mr. Dennis is a little elderly—"

"Jimmy!"

"Strike, if you must, this old gray head," he said, and winced exaggeratedly as if he parried a blow, "but think things over. You meet a good many eligibles here. Make hay, darling. Be a Maud Muller. My hay-ing time is briefer because my job won't last as long. 'Bye, got to get back to the grind. Be seein' you."

She was appalled, she was outraged. And her hands were tied. There was no one to whom she could talk except Dan and she shrank from confiding in him. And as time went on she observed Elise with anxiety. For if she, Jill, knew anything about the symptoms, Elise was falling in love, had fallen in love, with Jimmy.

It softened her, made her more generous, less sharp with Mary, more companionable with Sally, more considerate of her uncle. She was even affectionate toward Jill, coming into her room evenings, late afternoons, talking to her, leading, as often as possible, the conversation around to Jimmy. Jill was in despair. She tried to warn her. She said all the casual things as casually as she could. She said that Jimmy was great fun, never serious, lighthearted, light-minded. But Elise ate it up as if she were listening to praise.

Jimmy, Jill acknowledged, played his hand very well. He was charming to Mary, and had become excellent friends with Sally. He did the work required of him and did it well. Mr. Dennis was pleased with him. He had not had the response from H. Chester which Jimmy gave him. Jimmy was an encouragement and a spur. He supposed it was because Jimmy himself wanted to write; and would write someday.

Mr. Dennis said all this at the lunch table and Jimmy answered solemnly, "When my ship comes in," and winked at Jill.

She taxed him with it afterward.

"When your ship comes in! Jimmy, you're the laziest living white man. Save your salary, put it away; by the time you are through here you'll have enough to live on with reasonable comfort for some time and then you can write."

"Look here, Jill," Jimmy told her, "some people work better under the spur of necessity. They work like nailers, hunger sharpens their creative faculties. But there are others who can't work that way. I'm one of them. Give me freedom from any material care, any responsibility, any necessity for earning a living, and I swear to you by all you hold sacred that I'll turn out good stuff. Stuff that will sell. It will more than sell, it will get me a reputation."

For once in his life he was perfectly serious. He went on:

"A few geniuses find that they burn brighter when there isn't any heat in the attic. I'm not made that way. I can do a lot better work in a quiet library with the butler answering the telephone. Don't condemn me for it, Jill. It's the way I'm made. Someday I'll prove it to you!"

The rest of the summer sped to its close. Outwardly

everything was serene enough. The girls went on their usual rounds of parties, and Jill went with them. Evenings Jimmy went along as often as not, commandeered by Elise. Daytimes he was closeted with Mr. Dennis. Dan came over when he could. No more mention was made of the South American project.

In late September Sally celebrated her eighteenth birthday. Her grandfather gave her a big party and the weather held clear, with a lingering warmth by day and cool nights. There were forty people for dinner, and a hundred or more afterward for dancing and supper. Cars came from all over the Island, from town, Westchester, Connecticut. All the arrangements had been left in Jill's hands after consultation with Mr. Dennis. He had been leaving more and more to her as time went on. She talked with gardeners, orchestra agents, caterers, planned the decorating and the girls' frocks. The party was by way of being a debut, although Sally had one more year at the finishing school, a year which would be devoted to the domestic and cultural subjects, housekeeping, art appreciation—the usual polishing off. She had fought against that last year, but her grandfather had been firm. She should have her birthday-debut party, at eighteen, but for one more year she must attend school.

Sally's frock was utterly successful. Jill had steered her away from the sort of ultrasophisticated thing she'd set her heart on and in the end Sally acknowledged that Jill had been right. In white, with strewn stars of silver, bouffant skirt, girdled in delphinium blue and silver, she had never looked prettier, and knew it, with her hair caught up and pinned with a diamond star which had been her grandfather's gift. Mary, permitted to attend, and to stay up as long as she liked, fared almost as well. She was brown and hard, she had lost weight and her skin had cleared. She had a new haircut and a charming little frock, not too youthful nor too mature, and she had never looked so well.

It was a very good party. Late that night, sitting out in the garden with Jimmy on one side and Dan on the other, Jill yawned. She said, "Sorry, boys," apologetically, "but I'm dead tired . . . this *has* been an occasion! It will be over soon and I hate to think of it—after all the work. The interviews, the smoothing down of servants, the trips to town."

"It's a knockout," said Jimmy.

Dan said, "You did a good job." He had come with some reluctance, parties weren't in his line, but he had enjoyed himself although he hadn't been able to monopolize Jill.

"No one," mused Jimmy, "got very drunk."

"Why should they be drunk at all?" asked Jill in astonishment. "You know Mr. Dennis by now. He

183

wouldn't serve anything, that is, not to the youngsters. The older men of course . . . in the library."

"Some of the kids found their way in," reported Jimmy, grinning. "I know I did."

Jill said with distaste, "One of the men, a friend of Elise's, from town, arrived here in a state of perfect plaster. I had the devil's own time with him. He wanted to go out and look at the moon."

"And did he?" asked Dan.

"He did."

"What happened?"

"I slapped his face," said Jill.

"How old-fashioned," commented Jimmy. But Dan asked quietly, "Point him out to me, will you, Jill?"

"The silent menace," said Jimmy.

"Oh, his wife took him home," said Jill. "She told me she always took him home after he was slapped. I told her I wished she'd co-operated before!"

She leaned back against the rustic bench and sighed. She smoothed out the pale-green skirt of her new frock and rumpled her red hair with careless hands. Jimmy said, smoking reflectively:

"I've a dance with Sally. Must get going. Kid looks pretty tonight, doesn't she? Hates like thunder to go back to school. Can't say that I blame her."

Jill said idly, "I suppose Mr. Dennis thinks that this last year will teach her to handle money. She's going to take a business course as well as the others, I believe."

"What money?" asked Dan.

"Her own. She came into it tonight. On her eighteenth birthday. From her parents, you know. Mary won't have her share till she's eighteen. I believe there's considerable. Somehow," said Jill, yawning again, "I can't worry about Sally. She has a cool head on her little shoulders."

Jimmy had risen, tossed his cigarette away, and was strolling off. A moment or so later Elise came across the lawns toward them. She was wearing black, very low cut, very streamline. She said, "Hello, you two. Seen Jimmy?"

"He went to dance with Sally," Jill answered.

"He won't get near her," Elise prophesied, sitting down beside them, "she is knee-deep in callow cubs." She stretched her arms, clasped them behind her head. "It's been a lovely party," she said, "and all due to you, Jill."

This was, Jill felt, unusual generosity. She said:

"Thanks. It was fun, planning. Were you satisfied with the orchestra, Elise? I was uncertain at first. I had half a dozen to choose from, you know."

"They're fine," Elise answered. "Why don't you two run away and dance? If you see Jimmy tell him he'll find me here."

As Dan and Jill walked off, Jill said suddenly:

"I think Elise is serious about Jimmy."

"Oh," said Dan, "I wouldn't worry. Summertime stuff, you know. Doesn't mean a thing. And Jimmy has a lot of that well-known charm. Look at him now exercising it on little Sally."

They were passing the place where the platform was laid over the lawns and where a dozen couples still danced. Sally, her white, starry skirts swirling about her, was laughing up into Jimmy's face. She saw them, waved, stopped.

"Come on," she suggested, "the floor's just getting good."

"Elise is looking for you, Jimmy," Jill reported, "back in the rose garden."

"He's occupied," said Sally. She made a little face at her partner and he made a worse one at her. They smiled at Dan and Jill and moved away to the heady beat of the music.

"Now I wonder!" cried Jill, standing stock-still.

"What?"

"Nothing. Too absurd. I just remembered something. But I can't believe it. Dan, I'm dead. I wish everyone would go away. Let's hunt up some coffee. Perhaps that will pull me through the rest of the night," Jill said, her momentary anxiety dismissed and forgotten.

186

CHAPTER XI

SHORTLY after Sally's party the Dennis family returned to town. The exodus was accomplished with speed and ease, Jill accepting her share of the burden. During the first fine crisp week in October Sally and Mary returned to school. The night before school opened Sally wandered into Jill's room and made definite complaint.

"It's too silly," she said, "isn't it? I mean, going back to school. At my age!"

"At your age," Jill reminded her, "a lot of girls are just entering college."

"But I'm not," Sally pointed out, "and why should I? Never wanted to. It's all right if you want to go in for something, teaching, business, a profession, but it's idiotic if you don't. Waste of time and money. I'm not in the least athletic in the sense of going in for violent exercise in a big way. I'm not a student and I have plenty of friends without looking around for more. No, Jill. This further education is just plain goofy."

Jill said reasonably:

"Your grandfather wants you to learn how to run a

187

house properly, he wants you to interest yourself a little more in books, and the business course will help you a lot, Sally, in handling money."

Sally interrupted, wrinkling her little nose:

"Why should I learn to housekeep? There'll always be someone to do it for me."

Jill looked at her in despair . . . and in a sort of pity. How could Sally be so sure? Didn't she realize there might be a day when there wouldn't be anyone to "do" it for her? Jill thought, What does it feel like to be so terribly secure? And thinking, realized with a little shock, not wholly pleasant, that she herself had reached during the last six months a feeling of security, a sense of being surrounded by ease, and dependence, for agreeable, smooth living.

Sally was talking, with marked petulance:

"I can't interest myself in books if I don't like them, can I?" She regarded Jill with resentment. "Oh, I like to read," she went on, "to be amused—but the sort of highbrow things Grandfather wants me to take an interest in—well, I can't and that's flat. As for handling money, I'm not so dumb . . . besides what are banks and brokers and lawyers for, anyway?"

Jill said, carefully, "Banks have been known to fail, brokers to run out on you, and not all lawyers are—"

Sally shook her head.

"I've heard all that before," she interrupted, "and

anyway I don't know what good I'm doing sitting here crabbing. You can't get me out of school. Or can you?" She looked at Jill with her yellow head cocked on one side, like a very pretty, inquiring bird. "I wonder! You know, you have a lot of influence with Grandfather," she said.

"I?" asked Jill, in genuine surprise.

"Of course. He depends on you—a lot."

Jill said, "After only six months? It isn't possible. But even if I had all the influence in the world, Sally, I wouldn't try to get you 'out,' as you put it. Look, it won't be so bad, honey. Just a tour around galleries, and attendance at concerts, and plays and things you'll really like. The housekeeping part will be fun. They've such a marvelous setup—kitchen and tiny apartment all complete, and," she said smiling, "I understand they've borrowed a baby as well."

"Squawks," said Sally briefly.

"Surely not all the time?" exclaimed Jill.

Sally said, "If you think I'll enjoy the business course, with typewriters and adding machines, you're crazy. Moreover, there's an old fluff that teaches finance. You should see him, complete with gray beard and spats in season. One of the Folsom girls took it last year, she said it was a riot: graphs and stocks and bonds and a game of Monopoly when the interest waned. I don't understand men who give these courses," added Sally, bored to extinction; "if they know so much about money, why don't they go out and make it instead of teaching in a finishing school?"

After a little more grumbling she departed and Jill sat there thinking. She had not realized that she had influence with Mr. Dennis . . . oh, to a certain extent of course. But Sally seemed to think that she could influence him on important matters. It gave her a curious sense of power, an illusion of importance herself, and while she tried to laugh and shrug it off, she found herself thinking more and more about it and even, cautiously, testing it out.

She changed Mary from one dancing school to the other, persuaded Mr. Dennis to increase the child's dress allowance, and proved Sally's contention in other rather trivial ways. She found, as winter approached that Mrs. Gadman came to her on housekeeping matters more often than she did to Mr. Dennis, after knocking at the library door and being told, a dozen times, "That's all right, ask Miss Jill what to do."

Mrs. Emory, coming to dinner, took Jill aside afterward.

"My child, you've worked wonders. Mary is presentable, she's even quite pretty, and her manners are vastly improved. And Sally's charming. My dear old Charles beams upon you as if he had created you himself. And he seems very happy with the Bates boy." She laughed, her black eyes snapping. "You haven't persuaded young Bates to take Charles night-clubbing yet, have you?"

"Heavens, no!" Jill replied.

"Well, it's all worked out wonderfully," stated Mrs. Emory with satisfaction, "even Elise seems less like a weak cup of tea with a drop of vitriol in it and more like a human being. I congratulate you."

Jill said, embarrassed, "I wish you wouldn't. I haven't done anything. You make me sound like Little Sunbeam, the Indian Control, or Pollyanna's maiden aunt."

"Don't be so modest, my child. I don't believe you feel that way really. I'm sorry I couldn't come to Sally's party. They tell me it was perfect; no contretemps, no young men swept out from under the table in the early morning, no unconscious young women picked off the hedges. But, as I wrote you, I decided to go abroad in a hurry and went—just that way. And of course I didn't return till October."

Jill said, "We all missed you."

Mrs. Emory tapped her cheek with her finger. She said, contentedly, "It was a good day for the Dennis family when I thought of you and sent you over to see Charles. Jill, you aren't thinking of getting married, are you? For mercy's sake," cried Mrs. Emory in dismay, "the chit is blushing."

"What *is* a chit?" asked Jill, laughing. "I always

thought it was something you signed at bars or clubs in the Orient when you'd run out of money."

"Chit," explained Mrs. Emory firmly, "is what you are. Answer my question."

"No, of course not," said Jill.

"You don't sound convincing. Please, for all our sakes, eschew the orange blossoms for a time. Charles really depends on you, and trusts you. And I mean this. He told me so. And there's Sally to marry off properly. Mind you, it's properly. And after her Mary—"

"How about Mr. Dennis?" inquired Jill wickedly.

"Leave him alone," advised the old woman, "if I won't have him no one else shall—or is it may? My syntax slips as I grow older. I find myself 'don'ting' in the wrong places and given to quaint, homely old-fashioned ain'ts. It's nice, like cutting corset laces. But you don't know anything about corset laces. Anyway, corsets don't lace, nowadays and they are foundation garments, at the best."

"Sally," announced Jill calmly, "has had three proposals. All unsuitable."

"Three! How'd you find out!"

"She told me."

"What did she do about them?" inquired Mrs. Emory.

"Apparently she said, 'I'll let you know by the first

of the month.' She was too excited to refuse and too cautious to accept. All three happened at her dance. She consulted me afterward, at about four in the morning. It seems she's not interested in any of the men . . . the oldest was twenty-eight, practically a graybeard. But at the same time to have her first proposal turn out triplets, so to speak, was pretty keen. She couldn't bear to say no outright. But I pointed out to her that it would be awkward or at least slightly inconvenient to be engaged to three men at the same time. So she wrote them all nice little notes. I read them. They sounded exactly as if she were declining an invitation to tea!"

"Sally," prophesied Mrs. Emory, "will garner ten times three proposals before she is done. She's very pretty, and with all that money—"

"Not hard to take," agreed Jill. She added diffidently, "I don't mean to be impertinent, Mrs. Emory. But I've heard so much about the money. It might be ten thousand or ten million . . . could you tell me . . . I mean . . . oh, dear," she said, flushing, "it sounds so terribly prying no matter how I ask it."

"Why shouldn't you ask? After all, Sally's more or less in your charge, and if I carried a pocketbook around with me I'd want to know how much was in it, especially if it belonged to someone else. When her parents died there was about half a million dollars for the children. It's been increased by interest, I expect, despite the difficulty of investment in the last few years. The majority of it came from the children's mother. Of course Edgar had something of his own and earned a good income as well. But his wife, Patty Lawrence, was an only child and had inherited a good deal. Therefore, conservatively, a quarter of a million to each of the children on attaining the age of eighteen."

"I wish," said Jill helplessly, "that I hadn't asked! I was inclined to regard the three proposals as just tribute, but now I'm not as sure!"

"Don't worry," advised Mrs. Emory. "Sally will be loved for herself one of these days and if two hundred and fifty thousand comes with her she—and her husband—will be none the worse for it . . . I hope."

A few days later Jill was entertaining her friend Helen Elliott at tea. Helen, dark, sparkling, overthin, drank two cups and ate three cakes and looked about Jill's room enviously.

"You sure are sitting pretty," she commented, "when I think of the way we used to live. Can't get me a job, can you?"

"I'm afraid not," said Jill, "wish I could."

"Oh well, something will turn up. You got Jimmy in here," she added carelessly, "didn't you?"

"Not exactly. I mean Mr. Dennis met him through me and liked him. But I had nothing to do with his taking the place of the secretary who left. . . ."

She said nothing about the circumstances of H. Chester's leaving. It was wiser not. So far as she knew, even Mrs. Emory did not know unless Mr. Dennis had told her. But Mrs. Emory had not mentioned it, if he had.

"Tell me about yourself, Helen."

"Nothing much. The tourist camp job was swell while it lasted. I nearly married a hobo," volunteered Helen calmly.

"Helen!"

"Oh, a de luxe hobo. It was tempting. Feast one day and famine the next. But then I'm so used to it that it wouldn't have been much of a novelty. He was, as a matter of fact, a university professor who got bored with teaching the young idea to shoot, the wrong way, and took to traveling around in boxcars or whatever you call 'em . . . and listening to how the other half lives. He's writing a book."

Jill asked, "Haven't you saved anything?"

"Lord, no. What's come over you? You never talked like that before. Of course not. There wasn't enough salary to put in your eye, but food and lodging was free and it was an elegant climate. After I got back I got the tearoom hostess job. Terribly dull. Quit of my own accord. But I can manage. I'll try some sales job or other during the holiday rush. Thanks for putting me on to Mrs. Larsen. She's a marvel. Never saw such a face in my life. How do you suppose Larsen likes looking at it day in and day out? I expect to get back to Florida in January . . . Meantime, how's your exchequer?"

"Rolling. I can lend you some. Would a hundred help?" asked Jill.

"Help! It would practically put me in the millionaire class."

"All right," Jill said. "I'll get it out of the bank and send it to you."

"So you have a bank!"

"Well, a savings account. Not much. Of course I don't need my salary, I mean I need very little of it. I've my winter clothes bought and paid for and I'm under so little expense. I put most of the salary in savings, for a while."

"What did you do with it then, buy a yacht?"

"I invested it," said Jill, a little indignantly.

"Jill! You bloated bondholder!"

"No . . . but . . . well, I met a man last summer at the Island. He explained that while the market was in no condition to give me a big profit I could realize something. After all, the savings bank interest isn't much . . . I could get six, seven, even eight percent and be quite safe, he said. So I've sent him one hundred a month and put fifty in the savings bank and kept fifty. You can't buy a controlling interest," said Jill, "at one hundred a month!"

"If I were you," said Helen, "I'd put it all in the bank. But if you were I . . . that sounds a little confused . . . I'd blow it on something. It would worry me to be that rich! I'm not used to it. I've got so if I can't live from hand to mouth my appetite's ruined. Hunger being the best sauce."

Jill said thoughtfully, "I used to feel that way. I don't any more. It scares me to think of ever being anything approximating hungry again."

"You're spoiled," said Helen. "And you used to be such a good egg, carefree and lighthearted. All this security will ruin you yet." She looked at Jill affectionately. "Your only out," she said, "is to marry the richest man in seven counties and let him do the worrying. Then I'll apply for the job of eating the crumbs from your table. Scavenger, that's me."

Her brief encounter with Helen and that young lady's attitude toward life brought home to Jill more sharply how much she herself had altered in a few months. She told herself stoutly that the alteration was for the best. Dan would think so certainly. Hadn't he deplored her earlier viewpoint, urged her to solidity of purpose?

It was therefore something of a shock to her when he came to see her shortly thereafter and listened to her mirthful account of Helen without answering merriment.

"You don't think it's funny," Jill said reproachfully, "I thought you'd be proud of me, the way I've changed."

"But have you, Jill?"

She said, uneasily, "I'm trying to save. I've a new set of values. I'm beginning to appreciate solidity, purpose."

"What purpose?" he asked instantly. "A desire to be safe, to entrench yourself in an easy job and with a bankbook?"

She cried, "Dan, I don't understand you at all!"

"I'm afraid not," he said regretfully. He added, "When I used to talk about purpose to you, Jill, I didn't mean just this . . . not material purpose."

She said, "Dan, I'm happy here. I like it."

"I know. That's why I hesitate to ask you."

"What?"

"To come to South America with me . . . next week."

"Dan." She was breathless, silenced. They sat together in the small drawing room of the Dennis house. They were quite alone. A log burned on the hearth with a hissing sound and the picture of Sally and Mary's young mother looked down serenely from over the mantel, a lovely girl's face, as remote from tragedy as a Sunday morning in June.

Dan said, "I'm going back. It's a good job, a long

one and hard. I won't make much money. There'll be hardships. You'll have to fight a lot of your battles alone, Jill, I won't always be there. There'll be times when I'll leave you for weeks on end. You'll be by yourself, in a strange country, and a wild part of it. You'll do most of your own work without any of the usual conveniences. You'll hear a strange tongue. You'll have no one but me. There won't be many American women where we are going and most of them will be a lot older than you. But if you love me—"

She said, her heart pounding. "Oh, Dan, I don't know, I don't know!"

"You don't know if you love me!" he asked, frowning at her in his concentration.

She cried, "I do love you, Dan. I mean . . . you're the only person . . . all this summer I've known . . . no one but you, Dan. But . . ."

"You don't love me enough?" he asked.

She looked at him miserably, seeing beyond his loved and attractive face the miles of water, the strange camp, the place she couldn't picture in her mind, but somehow imagined she knew . . . hard, busy men, a makeshift home, alien suns and storms, a language she did not know, women with whom she had little in common, a difficult way, and Dan absorbed in his work, to which she must always come second.

He said slowly:

"I suppose so. Before you came to the Dennises I thought, She's a gambler, she gambles on herself, risks a lot, takes it with a laugh. If she came to love me she might gamble on me, with me, too. But I wasn't sure. But now"—he shook his head—"you would be afraid to risk anything again, wouldn't you? You've been seduced by soft living, by ease."

She said hotly, "Dan, you're so unfair. It isn't that. But it wouldn't be right—for you or myself—if I were to say yes and go and then find—"

"That you couldn't make good?" he asked abruptly.

"What about yourself?" she inquired angrily.

They looked at each other as enemies look. And then he made a short impatient sound, rose, came to her, swept her out of the chair in which she sat and into his arms. His arms were exceedingly strong, they held her with no chance of escaping. He kissed her, half a dozen times, hard, almost angrily, taking her breath and bruising her lips.

When he let her go he said, "That's for good-bye."

"Oh, Dan." She went to him again, held him, her hands on his arms. "Dan, I wish," she said truthfully, "that I had the courage."

He said, "You don't love me enough, my dear. I wouldn't take less than enough. I want more than enough, I'm afraid."

She said, "You—you'll come back?"

"Oh yes," he said, "I'll come back someday. To see if you've changed—again."

"And you?" she said, and began suddenly to cry, "you'll change."

"I won't change," he said, and his dark brows drew together. "I'll grow, God willing, but I won't change."

She said, "There'll be someone else."

He laughed at her, without pleasure. "Perhaps," he said. "I hope so. Would you have me remember you all your life and mine and want you and long for you and be without . . . That's pure selfishness. Let me go, say 'I hope I never see you again.' It will be easier that way."

She said, "I don't want you to go. Oh, Dan, if there were a place for you here. A good job. One you could advance in. Then—"

He said, "Jill, there is just such a job. I was offered it, not long ago. But I'm taking the other. Less pay, more work, harder . . . and out of the country."

Her tears were dried. She looked at him in rebellion, the red hair wild about her pointed face, her green eyes blazing.

"You had the chance . . . and you wouldn't take it!" she cried. "Not even if it meant me!" she cried.

"Yes," he said, "not even if it were to mean you. It is a desk job, Jill. It has to do with factories and mechanical things and routine. It promises advancement. I'd grow fat and old and stodgy sitting there. I'd hate it. It isn't my work, it will never be."

She said, "You called me selfish!"

There was nothing more to say. They had come to a dead-end street. They went over and over it again. And Jill kept saying, flushed with anger, with pleading:

"But we could be so happy . . . we could have an apartment somewhere or a little house . . . we'd be *safe.*"

He said, "I don't want to be safe. Not in that way. The only real security, Jill, comes from within. Through work that means something to you. Or love. You haven't found either."

She said, "When you come back—"

"That will be a long time. You'll have forgotten me, Jill."

"No," she said, "I won't forget you. I'll remember you and think, If he hadn't cared more for his profession than for me . . ."

"That isn't fair."

"It's fair enough."

Elise came in with Jimmy. They had been to the theater. Jimmy, quick to observe the air of emotional tension in the room, and Jill's too-bright eyes and flushed cheeks, was voluble and tactful in the extreme.

He suggested a raid on the icebox. They went, the four of them, to the kitchen, tiptoeing with caution in order not to wake the Gadget, who slept upstairs but was rumored to hear mice in an apartment house eight doors away, so keen was her hearing. And after a while Sally came yawning into the kitchen, a white woolen bathrobe belted about her little person and her hair tied back with a ribbon. She had gone to bed early because of a headache and here she was, sitting on the kitchen table, gnawing a chicken bone, the picture of health, laughing with Jimmy and ignoring Elise who sulked over a glass of milk. Elise had been none too pleased at Jimmy's including Dan and Jill in the icebox expedition, and the addition of Sally was the last straw so far as she was concerned.

Later Jill went with Dan to the door. It was the only moment she had alone with him, and the last.

"Shall I see you before you sail?" she asked.

"Think not. Better not," he said.

"Dan, you'll write? You'll let me know where you are?"

"I suppose so," he told her. "I'd be just that much of a fool—looking for your letters, living on them." He added angrily, "I'd give my right hand if I didn't love you, Jill."

He was gone, down the steps and away. She looked

through the clear glass of the door. "Dan," she said, aloud.

"Want me to fetch him back?" inquired Jimmy, at her elbow.

She jumped. "Oh, how you scared me," she said crossly. She was silent a moment. She was tired, worn out with conflicting emotions. Upstairs her pleasant room awaited her, rosy with shaded lights and drawn blinds, fruit juice in a thermos beside her bed, the bookstand filled with new novels, the eiderdown turned back and the crisp, colored sheets. . . .

"No," she said, "I don't want him back."

CHAPTER XII

LACKING Dan, discovering unhappiness, was like an icy shower after you've become accustomed to immersion in a warm and scented bath. Jill could not brace her-self, her emotional circulation was impaired, and she went about her daily routine feeling as if she had become, permanently, chilled.

The girls noticed it, even Mr. Dennis spoke one day of her listlessness and pallor. There was no one to whom she was close enough to talk except Jimmy. And to him she said nothing until he asked her.

"What's become of Noble Suitor—you know, the Boy Engineer?"

She started to reply lightly, "Hadn't you heard, he ran off to South America?" but to her horror she found herself in tears. Fortunately she and Jimmy were alone in the library.

Jimmy, with a cautious glance toward the door, put his arm around her.

"Here, buck up, what's happened?"

She said, after a moment, drawing herself away and regaining her lost control:

"It doesn't matter. I'm an idiot. He went off on a South American job, Jimmy."

"And didn't ask you to go along? Go ahead, tell me; after all, I've been the old safety valve for some time, Jill."

"He asked me," she admitted.

"Then . . . if you refused . . . why the weeps?"

"I'm a fool," she said angrily, "that's why. Jimmy, Dan could have had a job here, a good one. A chance for a future. Money enough to marry on . . . but he wouldn't take it."

"And you can't?" mused Jimmy.

She said:

"That's right, stick together. That's what Dan thinks, of course. But why *should* I take it—when I don't have to, when Dan could stay right on here in civilization and we could be so happy?"

"Blame yourself, Toots," Jimmy suggested. "You picked out a man with principles and a passion for discomfort. Don't think I don't sympathize with you. I see your point, only too well. But you'd better snap out of it. There are other men, not quite so noble or wedded to poverty and inconvenience. You can't," remarked Jimmy, "have your cake and eat it too. Or so I've been told. But I think there's something phony about that . . . I'll look into it one of these days." He patted her shoulder. "Cheer up, Jill," he advised, "Dan will come back, if you want him to—enough. And meantime, it's not so bad here, is it? Everyone likes you, you're happy, aren't you?"

"I suppose so," she said sorrowfully. "Of course," she swallowed, "I'm very happy."

Jimmy looked at his watch.

"I've got to run along and do an errand for the boss," he said, "see you at dinner. 'Bye."

When he had gone she sat forlornly in the library and wondered why things were so difficult. She supposed, resentfully, that she had been in love with Dan all along, ever since the return cruise trip. Not very much in love, perhaps, and fighting it certainly, but definitely interested, her curiosity engaged, and her senses responsive to the thought of him and to his presence. But now that he had gone away and she might not see him again the little had become much and life wasn't worth living and altogether things were in a muddle and she saw no way out.

At Christmas his first letter reached her. There were snapshots in it: Dan, looking straight at her, standing in front of a graceless little shack roofed with tin, in the broiling sun. He wore stained breeches, high boots, and a shirt open at the collar, and looked lean and dark and unsmiling. There were other pictures, mostly of the camp, and these she crumpled up in her hands and threw away. But she kept his, showing it to Mr. Dennis, casually.

"Isn't it nice? He has the work he wants," she explained. "His letter says he's had a rather hard time but things are beginning to shape up and he likes it. Of course he hasn't been there long. And he said, too, that he was so sorry to leave in such haste that he didn't get a chance to come say good-bye to us all."

"He's a splendid boy," remarked Mr. Dennis heartily, taking the picture in his narrow, long-fingered hand. "I'll be sorry not to see him again. How long does a job like that last, Jill?"

"I don't know," she replied vaguely, "a year, I suppose, or two— He didn't say."

Sally spoke from across the table.

"I thought he was swell," she said unexpectedly; "of course he didn't have much use for me. Thought I was about two and frivolous for my age . . . but I liked him a lot. Jill, you shouldn't have let him go away."

"I couldn't have kept him from going," said Jill, trying to laugh and almost succeeding.

The holidays came and went. Jill had lovely gifts, a check and a beautiful handbag from Mr. Dennis, lingerie from Sally, perfume from Mary, a knitted bed jacket from old Gadget, gloves from Elise, and from Jimmy an extravagant and effective bit of costume jewelry. Helen Elliott sent her a tinseled card and the announcement that she was resting between engagements and would Jill please come around.

Jill went, a few days after Christmas. Somehow it was a relief to get away from the big tree, the holiday atmosphere, the rooms a welter of tissue paper and ribbons, and climb Mrs. Larsen's stairs again. Mrs. Larsen, admitting her, was as ever, her currant-bun eyes just as dark and lost in doughlike flesh, her limp handshake just as Jill remembered it.

"Glad to see you, I'm sure," she said, a little on the stately side, "you will find Miss Elliott in your old room."

Jill went up the echoing stairs. There was Helen hunched up on the sagging bed Jill so well remembered, darning a stocking. She looked up as Jill came in.

"Hello, stranger."

Jill said, "The door was open so I didn't knock. Merry Christmas."

"I could do with merriment. Thanks for the stockings you sent. I'm saving them. Sit down, throw those things off the chair. How was The Larsen? Any complaints about me?"

"None. She seemed much as usual."

"I paid her—in advance, thanks to you. Wanted to

be sure of a roof. I can get along without feeding but not without sleeping."

"Thought you had a job. Your postcard said so; but not what it was."

"It lasted a couple of weeks. Medium, over on the dark side of town. Needed a receptionist and was willing to pay ten a week to the proper girl. Wanted education, gentility, and a belief in spirits. I must say it was easy to believe in the sort of spirits she frequently consulted. Otherwise, well, I wish I'd stuck it out, in a way it was marvelous. Terribly sad of course: such credulous people, little old ladies, elderly men, a bedraggled girl or two. Much to-do with bell ringing and tambourine clattering and Madame Sophronia going off into trances and talking in a bass voice."

"I knew one once, in Coney Island," said Jill reminiscently. "She was a good egg."

"Sophronia's a bad one. You pays your money and takes your choice. I couldn't bear the unhappy people who gave up two dollars to be duped and went away with their eyes shining. It was bad enough to let them in, and listen to the hopeful, anxious conversation, bad enough to have to dust and sweep the stuffy little place, and make appointments, but when she tried to press me into service when her daughter—terrible creature— wasn't available, I balked and quit. Never liked tambourines myself. It was just as well because shortly after I left the police got wind of some funny business about stocks. I don't know myself what it was all about, but it appears that Madame Sophronia had a husband with desk room somewhere and blocks and blocks of pretty printing on the nicest paper. So now and then, whenever she saw a chance she advised her clients, via Sitting Bull or someone, to buy whatever it was. And of course they didn't go to a broker, they went to the man she said was *her* broker . . . and that's that. I'm glad I pulled out, otherwise I would have landed in court too. I read it all in the paper and about died."

Jill asked:

"What about Florida?"

"Had a letter this morning. I leave the tenth of January by bus . . . if we don't get snowed in. At least it's a berth for the winter. Lord, I envy you a good job and no worries."

Jill said:

"That's right; sometimes I envy myself."

She looked around the room in which she had spent so many weeks. She saw the discolored walls, peeling paint and paper, the cheap scratched furniture, the dresser marked with cigarette burns. She saw the one window, the curtains a little dingier than the glass, and the carpet with the tear in it over which she had tripped so often. She thought, in a panic, I couldn't go back to it again, I *couldn't*.

She had lost the taste for adventure, the faculty of living from day to day.

"How are all the heavy boy friends?" inquired Helen negligently.

"Jimmy," replied Jill, "isn't a boy friend. He's all right. Mr. Dennis is awfully pleased with him. Of course his job just lasts till June but meantime . . ."

"What about Dan what's-his-name? You used to write about him a lot and last time I saw you you mentioned him every other minute. Clothes. Dan. Job. Dan. The Dennis estate on the Island. Dan. Et cetera, et cetera."

"He's gone away," said Jill.

"How come?"

Jill explained briefly, but Helen, her sharp black eyes curious, probed further.

"Look here, you're holding out on me. Quarrel?"

"No . . ." said Jill. She looked at Helen helplessly. She added, "He wanted me to marry him and go with him."

Helen said, "I see. Like him, don't you?"

Jill nodded.

"In love, I take it?"

"I suppose so," said Jill unhappily.

"But you wouldn't go. . . . Would you have six-seven

months ago, before you'd got your teeth into this Dennis outfit, so to speak?"

"I don't know," Jill said.

"Well, I do," said Helen. "I think you'd have gone." She folded her stockings, laid them aside. "It couldn't have been worse than you've experienced before and you'd have had him, in the bargain. You've gone soft, my girl. What will happen to you if you lose your present soft snap and have to scratch for a living?"

Jill looked at her friend. She answered slowly:

"Helen, I don't know."

Helen lay back across the bed. She said, her thin face sharp as a knife:

"We've been on our own too long, I guess. On the wing. Here today and gone tomorrow. There's a certain kick in it while it lasts. But you found a good safe nest with all the conveniences and modern heating, crawled in. You'd be afraid to fly again, Jill. I don't blame you. I've got to the point where I don't know that I'd welcome a permanent job, one that gave me clothes to wear, plenty to eat, and something in the bank. A regular, respectable job with regular, respectable hours. I'd be scared if I got it that I'd lose it. Because I'd know just what I'd have to go back to, you see. Always being on the bright side, trying to cultivate people who'd help you if they needed you, sort of cadging around for the next berth. It's been fun in some

213

ways and exciting, but we're out of drawing or something. I mean, we don't belong. We never did. Misfits. Born a little too soon or a little too late, lacking any special training. Look at the kids nowadays. My sister Gertrude, just out of business school, walked into a secretarial place as pretty as you please. My cousin Dora, out west, went to a vocational school and at nineteen is learning her trade in a decorator's shop, a big one, and being paid for it."

Jill nodded. "I know," she said.

"Take a chance," said Helen after a while, "cut loose from this particular corral. Go after your Dan. Grab him. I like the way he sounds. Wish I'd met him first— or even last—since you've said no."

Jill cried, "He hasn't been fair, Helen. He could have had work here, it would have paid him, enough for two to live on, and it had a future. But he has to go off to the wilds . . . I don't know why."

"He's an engineer, isn't he? I expect he has something he believes in," said Helen.

"He believes in stability," said Jill bitterly, "and a purpose. He was always after me because . . . because of the way I lived, from day to day. Then he turns around and reproaches me for not giving up the security of the one decent job I've ever had."

"Marriage," commented Helen, looking at the ceiling, "might be security too—no matter how little money you have. And stability, as far as that goes. And adventure."

Jill stared at her.

"You don't sound like yourself!" she said.

"No," agreed Helen sitting up, "I don't. I sound like a girl I knew, a little while before I met you. She had a chance to go to South America. Maybe it wasn't South America. Maybe it was just a safe, stodgy little town, and maybe her engineer was foreman in a factory. A dull job, you know, but it paid the rent. But it wasn't exciting enough. Keep house, mind babies? Not for her. So she said no too and there are times when she regrets it very much and other times when she doesn't give a damn."

Jill said, after a moment:

"Sorry, Helen."

"Don't be sorry for me. Be sorry for yourself. And stop looking at your watch."

"I've got to go," Jill told her. "The Gastons, neighbors of the Dennises on the Island, are giving a dance tonight. Sally's going of course. So am I."

"Chaperon or guest?"

"A little of both," Jill replied. She pulled Helen up from the bed, kissed her cheek. " 'Bye, keep the chin up," she said, "and let me see you again before you go south."

She thought she knew Helen so well, she reflected,

walking back to the Dennis house. Halfway there she called a taxi. Sinking back against the odorous upholstery, she thought, I didn't know her at all really. Oh well, I suppose it was just a mood. We all get them.

The Gaston dance was fun. There were extra men, and Jill was grimly determined to have a good time. They danced in the big ballroom of one of the hotels, and there was plenty to eat and to drink. Sally was in constant demand. Jill kept her eye on her as much as she could. But it wasn't easy. Therefore when around one o'clock she looked for her again and did not find her she was not alarmed.

She found Elise, standing talking to a group of people in one of the reception rooms.

"Elise, have you seen Sally?"

"Not for an hour or more," Elise answered. "Why, isn't she around?" She detached herself from the group and drew Jill aside. "I'm bored to death," she confided, "let's find Sally and go home."

Elise, reflected Jill, was bored because Jimmy hadn't been included in the list of Gaston guests, and now as they made their way to the dressing room Elise was saying plaintively, "So silly of Jimmy not to come. I rang up the Gastons and they said, bring him of course, perfectly all right."

Sally was not in the dressing room. But one of the

216

Gaston girls was there, a maid on her knees before her repairing a tear in a ruffle.

"Oh, Vera darling," said Elise, "it's been a divine party. But we must go now and have been looking all over for Sally. Have you seen her?"

"Why, she went home about . . . it must have been over an hour ago," answered Vera, astonished. "Didn't she find you? She said she'd tell you, and swore she wouldn't let you come with her. She had a dreadful headache. When I saw you after, I thought that one or both of you knew but had stayed on as she wanted."

Jill felt a chill of apprehension. She looked at Elise but apparently Elise was unshaken by foreboding. She said merely, "No, she didn't tell us."

Later, after they had said good night to Vera, found her mother and her sister and made their farewells, Elise suggested, "I wish Sally had told us, it would have given me an out. I'd have gone along home gladly."

Downstairs at the car Jill spoke to the chauffeur.

"Did you drive Miss Sally home," she asked, "around midnight?"

"Why, no," he told her. "I haven't seen her, Miss Hamilton. I've been here all along, parked up the street."

"She must have taken a taxi," Jill told Elise, "but why?"

"Perhaps she couldn't find the car," said Elise sensibly. "What's the matter, Jill, you're shaking? There's nothing wrong with Sally. I've never known her to leave a party of her own free will before, but if she had a headache . . . and she's had them frequently lately."

"Yes, I know," said Jill absently. "I took her to Dr. Gordon and he couldn't find anything. We went to an eye man too . . . there's nothing wrong with her eyes."

She was thinking, What's happened to her? Sally was Charles Dennis's granddaughter, she had inherited a large sum of money, she was well known . . . there might be kidnapers. Jill shook herself. Her imagination was running away with her.

Elise had her key and they let themselves into the house. No one was about. Jill flew upstairs ahead of the other girl and into Sally's room. She opened the door without knocking. Lights blazed. The room was in utter confusion. And it was empty. There was no sign of Sally in the bathroom or the little living room. Jill ran back to the bedroom and snatched a note off the bed, just as Elise appeared in the doorway.

"Where is she?" asked Elise. She broke off. "What's the matter," she said sharply, "where's Sally?"

Jill's fingers opened and the note fell to the floor.

"Sally," she said with difficulty, "has eloped with Jimmy Bates."

CHAPTER XIII

THE rest of the night remained a kaleidoscope of noise, a blaze of lights, and a confusion of tongues in Jill's memory. More clearly than either she remembered Elise's blazing eyes, her uncontrolled rage. "This is your doing," Elise screamed at her; "how much did you get for it?" And then before Jill, horrified and indignant, could answer, she was out of the room, running through the corridors, pounding on Mr. Dennis's door. "Uncle Charles! Uncle Charles!"

The servants crept from their rooms into back halls to listen and speculate. Mary came, rosy from sleep, her heelless mules clacking, her eyes round with amazement. And Mr. Dennis came too, a bathrobe belted about his tall spare figure and his face more stern than Jill had ever seen it.

Sally and Jimmy were gone.

How had they gone? And where had they gone?

Presently Mr. Dennis, Elise, and Jill were in his library. Mary came to the door and listened, hugging herself for warmth. No one paid any attention to her.

Elise, her face, which Jimmy, very early in his knowledge of her, had likened to a cup of weak tea, contorted, looked at Jill, and Jill, clutching after the sanity of inner laughter, thought, If he could see it now he'd know the milk had curdled!

Elise demanded, "Uncle Charles, you've got to stop them!"

Her uncle said wearily, "My child, how can I? Unfortunately Sally has reached an age at which she may, legally, marry without parental or guardian's consent."

Mary spoke up. "Golly, this is pretty exciting. Of course," she went on importantly, "I knew she was crazy about him. He's been meeting her . . ."

"When?" asked Jill, in a small cold voice.

"Oh, she used to leave school. She said she had a headache, or she'd say she was going home for the afternoon. She got Grandfather to sign excuses for her . . . he didn't know what it was all about."

"I signed reports," said Charles Dennis.

"That's what you thought. You didn't read them, did you?" asked the round, excited youngster scornfully.

"Of course I did, Mary."

"And then she took them away—the reports I mean —and brought you something folded over to sign. I knew all about it," Mary explained, "no one else did. I found out by accident."

220

"Jill knew," said Elise nastily, "she arranged it."

"She did not. She was the one they wanted to keep it from . . . that is, after Grandfather and you. Because," Mary went on with her appalling candor, "they knew that Grandfather wouldn't want Sally to get married—he'd think her too young—and they knew that Elise was nuts over Jimmy."

"I was not!" cried Elise. "You—you hateful little . . ." She stopped and burst into tears. She sobbed, "Oh, what does it matter, what does it matter? I did love him. I thought that he . . . Sally! Sly, lying, scheming. She had the money," said Elise bitterly, "and so Jimmy—"

Mary said calmly:

"Sally bought a car a couple of weeks ago. That is, she gave Jimmy the money and—"

Mr. Dennis said, resigned:

"Heaven knows what they are planning, where they are." He added, "I can set the machinery for searching into motion but it won't do any good."

He looked old and haggard. He turned to Jill and said gently:

"I cannot blame you definitely, Jill, but I feel that if you had been a little more attentive you would have realized how things were working out . . . and prevented this. Sally," he added, "is so young. Eighteen!

And much as I like Jimmy he is irresponsible, he has no trade or profession, he . . ."

They listened, Jill and Mary, keeping their eyes turned from Elise who sat opposite Mr. Dennis at the desk her head on her arms, crying wretchedly, unashamed, her evening finery crumpled and disheveled.

Jill said:

"I give you my word, Mr. Dennis, I had no knowledge of this. If I had had I would have come to you." She looked at him, distressed, terribly disturbed, but her eyes were level and clear and honest. "I am fond of Sally," she added quietly, "and as you know, Jimmy Bates and I have been good friends. But I didn't approve of his coming into the house. Still what could I say?"

Elise cried, lifting her devastated face, "Don't believe her! She planned this—with—with him. If he succeeded in marrying Sally she'd get a cut. It couldn't have been unknown to her that Sally came into her money on her eighteenth birthday. And Jimmy Bates knew it. He's—*despicable!*" She flung around and faced her uncle. "You can have it annulled," she said, and Jill thought she could not believe that Elise could look so plain, her fair skin blotched, her eyes swollen, all her poise and manner vanished. "You can do *something!*" she cried. "It isn't fair to me."

Jill said, "Elise, I had nothing to do with it. I'd give everything I have in the world to undo it!"

Mary came farther into the room and put her arm around the older girl. She said stoutly, "It wasn't her fault, Elise. You've just never liked Jill. You hated her coming here and then you thought at first that Jimmy was crazy about her, and after that when you found he wasn't and that you'd made a bad mistake about your old clip . . ."

"Will you shut up?" screamed Elise. "Why do I have to listen to her insults, Uncle Charles?" she appealed.

Mr. Dennis said abstractedly, "Go back to bed, Mary, at once."

Mary went reluctantly. She said, over her sturdy shoulder, "Just the same it isn't fair, riding Jill like this. She told you she had nothing to do with it."

"She had everything to do with it," said Elise, after the child had gone.

Her uncle said, "Elise, you are making a spectacle of yourself."

She jumped up, spread her hands flat on the desk and glared at him. She said:

"I'm sick of you too. I'm tired of your charity and I'm sick of this stuffy house and of Sally and Mary . . . of all of you. I'd get out in a minute if I could. But I can't. Why? Because I haven't any money of my own and because I haven't been trained to work.

You! You keep me down with a miserable allowance, and never let me forget that I came here under a cloud. And then you take this—this creature in, off the streets, from heaven knows where, and pay her a fat salary to sit around and do nothing and to plot and scheme behind all our backs so that her former lover can marry Sally and run through her money! That's how smart you are, Uncle Charles."

She cried again, laughed, flung herself down on the leather couch in the corner, drummed her heels, shrieked.

Jill went over and slapped her smartly across the face. "Be quiet!"

Elise's screams died down, her sobs ceased. She panted, sitting upright, "You dare—why, you . . . !"

Mr. Dennis came over hastily and caught her wrists. He said, "Call someone," helplessly to Jill. He had never before in his life had to do with an hysterical woman.

But suddenly the Gadget was there. She had been there, Jill suspected, all along, in her sober gray flannel gown, with her gray hair done up in curl papers for the night. She appeared as if by magic, and she had a glass of water in her hand. She threw it full in Elise's face, and then as the girl shivered and shrank away, beating her hands together, Gadget put her arm around her. She said soothingly, "Come along, Miss

Elise dear. I'll see you to bed. We'll get your clothes off, and something warm to drink and something to make you sleep."

Elise said sullenly, her breath catching, "All right." At the door she turned and looked back. Jill was standing by the desk. She was very pale and perfectly composed. Against her pallor her red hair was startling and her eyes were the color of malachite.

Elise said:

"I have some rights. After all, I'm your own flesh and blood. If you don't get rid of her, Uncle Charles . . ."

Gadget closed the door quietly.

In the lamplit room Jill confronted her employer. He looked so stricken and old that she wanted to weep. She asked, steadying her voice:

"Will you believe me when I say that if I could have prevented this—?"

"My dear, I do not altogether blame you," he told her wearily. "You were, after all, rather young for responsibility. If you tell me on your word of honor that you had no knowledge of this . . ."

"On my word of honor, Mr. Dennis."

He said, sighing, "All right. It doesn't bring Sally back to us." He asked after a minute, "Jill, tell me truthfully, will he be kind to her? She's so—little. And I've failed," he said dully.

Jill wanted to go to him, put her arms about him, for comfort. She could not. She was sick with the humiliation Elise had caused her, she was hot with fury against Jimmy, against that little idiot Sally, but most of all against herself. Had not Jimmy in a sense warned her again and again what he meant to do, and had she not been deaf to that warning? She replied, after a moment:

"Jimmy's decent, Mr. Dennis. I am sure he cares for her."

Does he? she asked herself, does he? Would he . . . if two hundred and fifty thousand hadn't come with her?

Mr. Dennis said, "I must have failed or I would not have lacked her confidence."

"She—she fell in love with him," said Jill.

"I suppose so." He looked at her with lack-luster eyes. He said, trying to rouse himself, "I'm sorry . . . Elise is very uncontrolled . . . I had no idea . . ."

He was stricken silent, realizing how little he knew about any of those close and dear to him, about Sally, Elise, Mary even. He let his hand fall heavily on the desk. He said, "I find I'm an old man, after all."

The tears were bright in Jill's green eyes. She said, "It hasn't been your fault."

"No?"

He rose and looked at her. She thought, I know

what he wants to say but he's too kind and too just to say it. I'll have to say it for him.

So she said it, her heart heavy in her breast.

"I can't stay on of course. I mean you'd never feel quite sure that I hadn't had a hand in this. And Elise . . . . you know how she feels. It would be an impossible situation. And you can't," she added, with her red head held high and her lips shaking a little, "you can't . . . prefer me . . . to one of your own. So," concluded Jill, and an absurd sad formality, "if you'll accept my resignation—"

He said, "Jill, my dear, I'm sorry."

He had, she saw, accepted it.

When she was leaving the room, her shoulders squared, he called to her and she turned back briefly. He asked:

"What will you do?"

"There'll be other places," she assured him, "and I've saved quite a little. You mustn't worry about me." She added, "And after all it was in a way my fault. I'd like you to believe that because it will make you feel a little better—about my leaving, I mean. You were right. I *should* have seen how things were going. That was my job. I didn't. I was too busy having a very good time. Too much concerned with myself. If it hadn't been for me, Sally would have never met Jimmy Bates."

He did not answer and she went on up to her room,

to lie across her bed until daybreak, too tired for tears. She thought valiantly, Well, there'll be something else. She thought, I'll sell the oil shares. I'll live as economically as possible and I won't have to take just anything that comes along. She thought, If I could get my hands on Jimmy Bates . . .

She despised him, he was the lowest thing that crawled, a man who ingratiated himself with an inexperienced girl, who persuaded her to run off with him secretly, stealthily . . . a man who married for money.

She looked around her pleasant room. This would be the end of such surroundings. She felt her heart beat faster, accelerated by anticipation and memory. She thought, I'm too soft to go back to it . . . the uncertainty and the living from day to day.

She was alone in a house in which people stirred, whispered, in which doorbells tinkled and telephones rang.

Jill did not see Elise again. When dawn came she bathed and dressed and packed her things. Gadget went to school with Mary, good old Gadget, coming into Jill's room saying, "I'm sorry, Miss Jill."

So they all knew, then. What she had done, what she had left undone, and that she was leaving.

The doctor came and went. To see Elise, who was still prostrate, taken by fits of furious, weakening weep-ing; and to see Mr. Dennis, who, shortly after Jill had left him, had suffered a heart attack.

That, too, was laid at Jill's door. Once coming into the corridor, she heard Gadget talking to Elise, telling her that she couldn't see her uncle, that he was ill, and she heard Elise's ugly answer through the half-opened door of her room. "Well, if he dies, you can blame Jill Hamilton for that too."

Jill went back to her room, sickened with fright. She thought, Oh, not that! Don't let anything happen to him—please—please. . . .

She did not know what to do, whether to creep away without a word, a dismissed servant, a servant who had failed of her trust or whether to wait in a house she felt hostile to her, until word came that Mr. Dennis was better. The other servants avoided her. Gadget alone remained. She came to the room that afternoon and said:

"Mrs. Emory is here."

"Where?"

"Downstairs. She wants to see you. And," said Gadget, "it's in the evening papers. They are full of it. There have been reporters, telephones . . ."

They had driven all night, those two, in Sally's new, fast little car. And they had been married, in a border southern state which required no notice of intention to wed.

Jill went downstairs slowly, her hand on the polished wood of the rail. Reluctant to let go, reluctant to step down the last tread and into the drawing room. Mrs. Emory stood there, her face set and inimical. She remarked with belligerence:

"This is a pretty kettle of fish."

Jill said, "Mrs. Emory, I knew nothing of it."

"So I understand. Charles telephoned me this morning. When he could. But I'm not, it seems, to see him now," said Mrs. Emory. "He doesn't blame you. He made that clear. But I do," she said honestly. "I always shall. You should have kept your wits about you. Introducing that good-for-nothing boy into the house—and especially to Sally, who hasn't a brain in her head and who'd take any opportunity to escape from Charles and make her own silly life and spend her own money! I'm bitterly disappointed in you, Jill."

Jill said, "I'm sorry, Mrs. Emory. There's nothing more to say. I—I've been told pretty plainly what people think of me."

Mrs. Emory said, "I've heard that too"—it was evident that she had pumped Gadget dry—"and that Elise is mixed up in this. Well, if young Bates had married her, it wouldn't have mattered, but of course he wouldn't marry her. He knows on which side his bread is buttered. He isn't a fool."

She sat down suddenly, an old woman, broken by bad news.

"I don't give a snap of my fingers for any of them really—except Charles," she declared. She looked at Jill, the black eyes still bright with anger. "I can't forgive anyone who lets him down."

That was pretty bad. But it was worse, at dusk to be summoned into Mr. Dennis's room. There was a nurse there, a middle-aged woman who shook her head at Jill and said warningly, low, "You are not to excite Mr. Dennis."

Jill said, "If you knew how sorry I am. . . ."

The nurse had gone, but the door between Mr. Dennis's big room and the next was left open. He lay propped up against the pillows, his color bad. He said:

"I know. You mustn't blame yourself for—this. It isn't the first time. It won't be the last." He tried to smile at her. He said, "We have had word from Sally. They—they are married, all right. They are coming back."

"Here?"

"No," he said, his face darkening with pain, "not here. They will let me know where they are. They have their own plans."

Jill said:

"I will never forgive myself." She went close to the bed and looked down. She wanted desperately to fall on her knees beside it and put her cheek to the thin old hand. She had loved this kindly, generous man very much. She said, standing there, "And I will never forget you . . . and your kindness to me."

He said, "Jill, I'm deeply distressed it had to be like this." He lifted his hand, took a checkbook and a pen from the night table. He said, "I can't let you go—thinking that perhaps you might be in want. You have been a member of my family for a good many months . . . so until you find another position . . ."

She said, scarlet, "Please, Mr. Dennis, I couldn't. You have given me far too much already. I have plenty . . . more than I've ever had in my life." Her voice broke and she implored him pitifully, "I beg of you to leave me a shred of self-respect."

The nurse came in, and beckoned. She said, "Mr. Dennis must not exert himself further."

Jill went to the door.

"Good-bye," she said.

But he did not hear her. He was lying back with his eyes closed and the nurse was moving softly and competently about the bed. Jill closed the door quietly.

Her things were taken downstairs and Joseph called a taxi. Joseph's very back was disapproving. He could not forgive her, an outsider. She had come in, she had received nothing but kindness, Joseph was thinking, or so Jill believed, and she had caused nothing but worry and distress and heartbreak and illness. The taxi man came up for the trunk.

Jill was alone with Gadget in the hall. She said, and cried suddenly and forlornly as a child cries, "Oh, Gadget!"

"There, Miss Jill," said Gadget. She sniffed. She said, "Maybe it's all for the best. I liked Mr. Jimmy," she said stoutly. "I think he has the makings of a good man. We'll see. And don't be too worried about Miss Sally, I've known her since she was born. She has a will of her own, plenty of spirit, and at the bottom of her heart, common sense. Or wherever common sense is, in a person. And I do wish you luck. You'll keep in touch with me?" asked Gadget coaxingly, "and tell me how things are going with you?"

"I will," said Jill, "you've been—sweet."

In the taxi she told the driver.

"Just—drive around for a while . . . I haven't quite decided. . . ."

The driver, a little amazed, but not too amazed, for New York taxi drivers are used to almost anything in the way of requests from their fares, drove around, obligingly, skidding a little on the soft snow, turning to ice in the cold December dusk, while Jill considered her position.

She had money in her purse, she had good clothes and luggage. She had a little in the savings bank, and, for her, a lot in some sort of oil stock. She could realize on that. Meantime she must live as cheaply as possible and look for another place. She thought longingly of a good hotel with deft service and comfortable beds, plenty of windows and a bathroom with steaming-hot water, the ordinary luxuries to which she had become accustomed during the past months. And then she shook her head.

She tapped on the glass between her and the driver and when he slid it back and looked at her inquiringly she gave him Mrs. Larsen's address.

CHAPTER XIV

"WELL," exclaimed Mrs. Larsen, opening the door and admitting Jill, the burdened taxi driver and a blast of cold air. The exclamation held inquiry, welcome, slightly tempered with caution, and a faint strain of triumph.

"Bad penny," explained Jill, trying to laugh. "Here I am. For a while, anyway."

The taxi driver inquired gloomily:

"Where you want your trunk?"

"Yes," asked Mrs. Larsen, "where?"

Jill said hurriedly, "Any room you have vacant. I know Miss Elliott has my old room. Perhaps after she goes I could move up there. But meantime—"

Mrs. Larsen beckoned majestically and trudged ahead of Jill up the stairs. She said, "Second floor back is vacant. If you'd like to take it. . . ?" She paused inquiringly on the landing and Jill said, "Yes . . . anything . . . is Miss Elliott in?"

"Man came, took her out to dinner. She's a worse

gadder than you ever were," commented Mrs. Larsen disapprovingly.

Jill entered the second floor back. It was a comparatively large room luxuriating in mission furniture. There was a double bed. Mrs. Larsen turned back the covers and poked the mattress. "It's a good one," she said. She looked at Jill, her currant-bun eyes sliding. She mentioned the price. It was almost twice as much as Jill's other room had been. She added, "And the bath's next door. There's no one on the floor now except Mrs. Parsons and, she as you know, has her own. *And* parlor," said Mrs. Larsen firmly, for the benefit of the taxi driver. But that gentleman, bent double under the trunk, said plaintively, "Well, for Pete's sake, make up your mind, I can't stand here all day like a bloomin' express wagon."

"I'll take the room," said Jill hastily, the trunk thudded down on the carpet, and the driver went downstairs for the bags.

Presently Jill paid her fare, and added a generous tip. Mrs. Larsen's eyebrows went up. When the taxi driver had departed Jill said, sighing, "It is nice. I hope I can keep it."

The second floor back by no means resembled her quarters at the Dennis town or country house, but it was a decided advance on her poky little room upstairs.

It had two windows, a rocking chair with a plush seat, and a lace tidy, and it was, for Mrs. Larsen, clean.

"I hope so too," said Mrs. Larsen, lingering. Jill reopened her purse and extracted some bills. She said, "Two weeks—in advance," and Mrs. Larsen unbent. She said graciously, smoothing out the bills, "I am glad to see you back. Sorry that you lost your position . . . or didn't you?"

Jill said, "Well, not exactly. The—the girl for whom I was engaged as a companion got married. Oh," she added, "she married Jimmy Bates. You remember him, don't you, Mrs. Larsen?"

Mrs. Larsen said, "Well, I never" and "You don't tell me!" She regarded Jill, her large white face greedy with curiosity. She said, "I thought you and him were such good friends."

"We were," said Jill laughing, "but that's all."

"And how's that nice Mr. Hardy? There," said Mrs. Larsen, "is a fine man, polite and pleasant."

"He's away," Jill answered, "in South America."

"Oh!" Mrs. Larsen went to the door. She asked, "You'll be going out to dinner?" But as Jill did not answer immediately she invited, suddenly, overcome by Jill's change of fortune and two weeks in advance, "Or—would you do me and Larsen the pleasure? I've a nice pig's knuckle."

Jill shuddered. She did not feel like a pig's knuckle.

She felt like nothing on earth. She said faintly, "That's ever so kind of you, Mrs. Larsen, but I've a pretty bad headache. I don't think I'll eat anything tonight."

"Nonsense," said her landlady briskly, "toast and tea will fix you up. I'll have Selma bring you a tray . . . this once," she added carefully lest Jill think that her change of room boded additional service. "Selma," she added, "is new since you was with me. She's like all the rest, ingrateful," announced Mrs. Larsen darkly, while Jill looked up and smiled faintly at her choice of a descriptive word, "complains all the time about work. But she's strong."

Jill said, "Thanks so much, Mrs. Larsen. If you see Helen Elliott when she comes in will you tell her I'm—back?"

"I will," promised Mrs. Larsen, and departed, shutting the door.

Jill cast off her hat and coat, threw her handbag on the dresser, looked with rancor at her unopened trunk and bags, and flung herself on the bed. It was a bouncy bed, and sagged a very little. But it was a better bed than the one Helen would sleep in tonight, if a much worse one than any Jill had slept in since her departure from Mrs. Larsen's. Her head, she found, did ache. She was too tired to cry. She lay there in the blaze of the unshaded bulbs and closed her eyes and tried to think. But she couldn't. All she saw was Mr. Dennis's

238

white face, blue about the lips, and Elise's distorted features.

She said aloud, "Honestly, it wasn't my fault!"

Once she got up and looked in her purse for the snapshot of Dan and sat on the edge of the bed and regarded it. She said, "Laugh, darn you," to it bitterly but the face in the picture remained unsmiling, eyes squinted against the sun. She threw the snapshot on the floor, picked it up, shoved it under her pillow, rose, switched out the lights and lay down again. She should unpack. She would not—not now. She should not submit her suit skirt to wrinkling. She didn't care. She lay still with her arms crooked over her eyes. Nothing mattered. She had lost her job, the affectionate interest of Mr. Dennis and of Mrs. Emory, she had forfeited Mary's doglike devotion, Sally's growing friendship, Jimmy's amusing companionship. She had lost the easy ways of living, her little importance, her influence in what now seemed to her high places.

Selma, the new maid, fifty if a day, clumped up the stairs and banged on the door. Jill, waking from the light uneasy slumber of fatigue, rose and turned on the light and admitted her. "Hello," said Selma, without pleasure, "she sent me up with this."

She bore a battered tin tray covered with a dingy cloth, and on it a plate of toast, a pot of tea, a pitcher of milk, a few lumps of grayish sugar, and a spoon.

"Set it down there on the round table," said Jill, "and thank you, Selma." She picked up her purse, found a coin. "Oh my!" said Selma, awed. And went off with a cantering sort of gait, as if afraid that Jill would change her mind. At the door she muttered "Thank you" rather hoarsely, her small wisened face startled.

Jill thought as the door banged, It's just a habit I've got into. Well, I'll have to get out of it.

She sat down before the tray. The toast was burned but it was hot and buttered and the tea was scalding and very strong. She ate and drank and felt a little better.

When Helen came in Jill was unpacking. Helen opened the door on the heels of her knock, shut it again. She said:

" 'Home is the hunter, home from the hill . . .' "

"Shut up," said Jill crossly, "and help me unpack."

Helen came in. She wore her shabby little suit with an air and a shiver. She said, "It's rotten out. I hope Florida lives up to its reputation." She plucked a frock from one of the trunk hangers and commented, "Well, if worst comes to worst, I know a secondhand woman you can sell these too."

Jill said grimly, "Thanks, I'll hang on to them. They're assets in a job."

"Depends on the job." Helen put some lingerie in

the bureau. The drawer stuck and she said, "Hell," very thoughtfully. Then she sat down on the bed.

"What happened?" she asked.

Jill, sitting cross-legged on the floor sorting stockings, told her briefly. Helen listened, made few comments during the recital, asked a question or two and then whistled shrilly.

"Well," she remarked, "you certainly put your foot in it!"

"Up to the neck," agreed Jill glumly, with slight regard for her anatomy.

Helen suggested, "Cheer up. You've got some money."

"Not much. Some in the savings bank. The rest I put in that oil business. It pays monthly dividends but I think I'd better sell it."

"By all means," agreed Helen, "troubled waters. Oil —it all works out. What next?"

"Look for a job." Jill lifted her red head, regarded her friend, "How about Florida?" she cried.

"That," said Helen, "would be swell. If there's a chance. Could you plunge on a wire?"

"Yes," said Jill, "if I have to."

"Then I'll wire tomorrow. They had a second girl working with me last year. Maybe she won't come back."

Jill said, "I could wait on tables."

Helen got down on the floor beside her and began to pull things out of the small compartments of the trunk. She promised, "We'll find you something." She looked at her friend sidelong. She said, "Grin and bear it, you've been in tighter spots with not nearly as much capital. Tomorrow's another day. Something will turn up. Smile. You look as if the world had come to an end. What's the matter with you? Where is the old college spirit?"

Jill said, "I've lost it. I'm scared."

"Oh," said Helen, "I was afraid of that. Too many fleshpots. Well, thank God I don't know what it is to lead the life of luxury, so I don't miss it. Look, Jill, we'll have a swell time together, down in Dixie."

But on the tenth of January Helen departed for Florida by bus and alone. All the positions at the tourist camp were filled. There wasn't a chance.

"Look, suppose you come anyway," she suggested, "you can manage the fare and there'll be something down there, near by perhaps."

Two years ago, a year, and Jill would have risked it. Now she shook her red head. "No, I guess not, Helen. I'm sorry."

Helen said, "'Just for a handful of ribbon you left us' or something like that. I'm not up in my Browning any more. Not since I was thrown out of the Browning Ladies Society for nonpayment of dues." She grinned and smote Jill on the back. She said, "Look here, you'll get over this. At least I hope you will. I'll write you. And perhaps something will turn up."

After her departure New York seemed very huge and empty. They had spent most of their time together. Helen knew a few young men not too indigent. There'd been dinners and lunches and a movie or two. They'd had fun . . . while Jill looked for work.

There wasn't any. She went to the old places and to new, and nothing was forthcoming. In desperation, shortly after Helen left, she answered an advertisement for a lady's maid. She could manicure, set hair, mend lingerie. She had not taken a beauty course but once she had filled in in a very minor beauty shop and besides if you live alone with not much money you learn to take care of your hair and skin and hands. But when she reached the apartment on Fifth Avenue, and was waiting in the anteroom for the servant to announce her, she heard a familiar voice in the hall.

"Who rang, Peters?" and the servant's reply, "The young person who came in answer to Mrs. Hopkins's advertisement, Mr. Arden."

When the butler returned with word that Mrs. Hopkins would see the applicant, Jill was no longer there. She had fled as if pursued and all the way down in the elevator her breath was short, her color high, and her pulses pounding. So H. Chester had found himself another place. But surely Mr. Dennis had not given him a reference?

That night Mrs. Larsen called her downstairs. "A gentleman to see you," she shouted.

"Who is it?" Jill shouted back.

She had moved up to the room Helen had vacated. Mrs. Larsen had regretted the move very much. She had been a little colder to Jill at first, no more offers of toast and tea, but gradually she was thawing.

"I couldn't say," Mrs. Larsen replied.

It might be one of Helen's young men Jill went downstairs and walked into the parlor. There, beaming at her from behind his horn-rimmed spectacles was H. Chester Arden.

She said, "I never thought I'd see you again."

He laughed. He said pacifically, "Sit down. Ask me to sit down. I want to talk to you."

"I can't imagine," said Jill, standing, "what you have to say."

"Oh, come," he said. "It was I who lost the job and not you. An error of judgment. I did a very foolish thing. But, well," he said slowly, "after all my dear you had given me to understand—"

"Nothing," she interrupted coldly.

"That's what you say. Look. I heard your voice today, at the Hopkins apartment. I got Peters to describe you. He did it very well: pretty, he said, with red curly hair and green eyes, slender, seemed anxious to get the place. And I knew you'd left the Dennises, and why."

"How," she demanded, "did you know that?"

"Oh, I hear things." He added carelessly, "I suppose you know Sally and your old friend Jimmy Bates are living in town?" He named the hotel. "They are sailing for Europe within a week or so," he said.

She said, "I didn't know. How could I?" She looked at him a moment and suggested, "Hadn't you better go?"

H. Chester rose. He had been sitting on one of the velvet chairs while Jill had remained standing. Now he faced her. He asked, "Wouldn't you like to know how I found you?"

"It doesn't interest me," she said coolly.

He took a little red notebook from his pocket. He said, turning the pages, "Relic of the dear old days. I had your address in this, you know. Perhaps you'll remember giving it to me during our first interesting interview. I had very little hope that you'd be here again, but there was no harm in trying."

She said, "You've taken a lot of trouble for nothing. I don't really see the point of all this, Chester."

"Listen," he said, "you're out of a job. I don't know if Jimmy has—or will—reimburse you."

Oh, she thought, Elise! He's seen Elise—they were

always good friends and she could forgive him the business about the clip because of the way she feels toward me. Perhaps she was never very annoyed with him, perhaps she was sorry his plan miscarried.

H. Chester was still talking. "However, the fact remains that you are looking for a place. Lady's maid!" He shook his head. "Still," he added critically, "in one of those trick stage uniforms you'd be rather sweet."

"Will you go?" asked Jill ominously.

He said, "It doesn't pay much . . . eighty a month. And Mrs. Hopkins is difficult. You see," he told her confidentially, "she's nearing fifty and she was once very beautiful. However—" he shrugged—"I think I could influence her to give you the position . . . if you'd let bygones be bygones . . . we could," he suggested, "console one another . . . it might be amusing. . . . I'm her secretary," he added carelessly, "courier, manager, what have you."

Jill thought, It's easy to see how he got the place, and said rather nastily, "I suppose Mr. Dennis gave you very good references."

"He did not," admitted H. Chester. "As it happened, I didn't need any. Not in this place. And how about you?"

She said nothing. She had been given no reference. She thought, If I were to ask Mr. Dennis—at least he could recommend me on the grounds of decency and honesty. But she knew that she would not ask him. She knew that she would be prevented from seeing him, that her letters would be opened. She said, "If you don't mind, Chester, I've decided not to apply for Mrs. Hopkins's position."

"Just as you wish, but you're making things tougher for yourself than necessary. After all, I hold no rancor. You're being very silly." He added, looking around the ugly room, "Beggars can't be choosers. I found that out. And it does not look to me, my dear Jill, as if you were very affluent."

A moment later and the door had closed behind him. Jill went upstairs wearily. She thought, Well, that's out. Any avenue which led back to the Dennis household was out also; or to Mrs. Emory. She would, she thought, have to start from scratch. And aside from the Dennis position, what references could she bring? The stopgap jobs carried none with them; there had been so many of them and all so varied.

The holidays were over. Not even a temporary selling post was open to her. She tried for a permanent position in many of the big stores. But there was nothing.

Toward the end of January she wrote to the man who had sold her the oil shares. The letter came back stamped "Not known at this address." The January payment had not come in. She tried to call his office but the telephone had been disconnected. Finally recalling one of Helen's friends was employed in a brokerage office she rang him up and he came around to see her. He was a pleasant young man named Warren, serious and attractive.

She told him of her contact with the share-selling gentleman and the dividends which had rolled in . . . "royalties" he had called them. But Mr. Warren shook his blond head.

"Smells like fish," he commented. "I'll look into it."

A day or so later he telephoned her, regretfully. The shares were worth exactly nothing. With the money that came in from the gullible buyers the suave young man and his associates had paid the "dividends" on other shares. And now they had departed bag and baggage and the Federal Government was looking for them. "I'm afraid," he said, "you've been had."

"And how," said Jill. She thanked him, accepted an invitation to dine next week, and hung up.

So that was that.

There remained a little in the savings bank and she still had her clothes. They were rather summery for New York in winter. Thank heaven for the old tweed coat, shabby, but fairly warm.

Coming back from dinner with Mr. Warren who, if a little on the dull side, could still provide an adequate meal, Mrs. Larsen met her at the door.

"That Jimmy Bates rang you up," she said. "He

wants you to call him when you come in. I wrote down the number. I thought he was married," she said.

"He is," said Jill. She fairly snatched the slip of paper from Mrs. Larsen's damp hand and rushed to the telephone in the drafty hall and called Jimmy's hotel.

Jimmy answered. He said, "Jill . . . well, of all things! We've hunted high and low. That is, we've speculated on putting a personal in the papers. Then I thought—perhaps she's gone back to old Larsen's. How're you doing?"

"Swell," said Jill. "Oh, Jimmy, you—you wretch! I'd adore to tell you what I think of you but I'm so darned glad to hear your voice. How's Sally?"

"She's fine. Look, come around and have dinner with us tomorrow night, will you? We're sailing Saturday."

Two dinners in a week. That was something for the budget. Jill borrowed Mrs. Larsen's iron, pressed one of her pretty frocks, decided to freeze in a light coat, and to splurge on a taxi. She thought, I ought to read 'em the riot act but—

On the way to the hotel she thought, I wonder if Jimmy will remember that fifty I lent him. Perhaps if I get a chance with him alone I'll ask.

But she knew she would hate asking.

She was taken upstairs to the Bates suite. It was rather impressive. Sally ran out, caught her in her arms, kissed her. Sally looked like a million dollars— or at least two hundred and fifty thousand. She wore a sophisticated black velvet frock and her yellow hair was caught into curls at the top of her head. Her eyes were clear, happy, and friendly, and Jimmy beamed upon her as if she were his private creation.

They had cocktails and then dinner in the living room of the suite. And Mr. and Mrs. Bates talked so much for the first half hour that Jill had very little to say.

Once Sally said, "I'm so sorry about all the fuss. That Elise . . . if it hadn't been for her . . . Jill, we're both terribly sorry."

"That's all right," said Jill, "it doesn't matter. But you were very bad young people."

Sally said, "Grandfather would have raised the roof. It was the only way. I fell in love with Jimmy the first time I saw him."

Jimmy looked pleased if self-conscious.

Jill asked, troubled, "How is your grandfather?"

"He's better," said Sally. Her pert face sobered. "Elise blames me for that too," she said. "I do despise that woman, I always have! If it weren't for her we'd have gone back home until we sailed. But she made it impossible. I've been to see Grandfather every day. Jimmy too. He's— Well, he's forgiven us," said Sally, "I suppose. That is, he says so."

Jill said, low, "If you knew how I felt, especially after he was taken ill. I—"

Sally said swiftly, "Look, Jill, you mustn't blame yourself for anything. Grandfather doesn't. He told us to tell you if we saw you . . . but that was last week. He left for Florida yesterday with the nurse and Elise."

"Oh," said Jill. She thought, I'll never see him again. Her eyes, shifting from hazel to clear green, were suffused with tears.

Sally said, "Look, are you all right? I mean, after all we owe you so much . . . if there's anything we can do . . ."

"I'm fine," Jill said stoutly.

"Got a job?" asked Jimmy, sitting beside Sally on the divan holding her hand in his.

"Not yet. I don't have to, right away. I've saved a little."

She wouldn't take money in charity. Nor would she be paid, as Elise had said she would be. If Jimmy wished to repay the loan, that was different. But he had forgotten it.

Sally said, "Jimmy's so smart. He's found us a funny little villa—at Cannes. We're going to Paris first. Then there. In the spring we'll be in England. Jimmy's going to write," she said proudly.

"I will too," said Jimmy earnestly as if Jill had denied it. "I can—now. I know I can." He smiled at Sally and she smiled back. Jill thought, He is fond of her . . . he is; that makes everything better.

Sally said, "I wish you'd come to visit us, Jill, it would be grand."

That was a laugh. A little later, when Sally had gone into the bedroom to find the pictures of the Cannes villa and the house in Sussex which they were going to take for the spring season, Jimmy and Jill were briefly alone. She said soberly:

"Jimmy, I'd grown to hate you, almost. How could you do a thing like that?"

"It was the only way," he told her.

She said, "If I thought that the money—"

"Listen," he said, "I'm crazy about her. She's a sweet kid. We'll be happy. We're bound to be."

She agreed, "Yes, perhaps, but if it hadn't been for the money—"

"Of course not," he said honestly. "Who am I to support an eighteen-year-old wife, or any wife for that matter? I couldn't support myself! But I swear to you, if I hadn't been crazy about her I wouldn't—"

"I'd like to believe that, Jimmy."

"You can. Look, I'm grateful to you—I can't tell you how much. I wish I could prove it."

She said, "You can prove it by being a decent husband to Sally, Jimmy, and that's the only way you can."

He said, "I will. You'll see. And I'll write. And sell. This will give me my start. I wasn't cut out to sweat it out in poverty and uncertainty, Jill. Not my fault. It's the way I'm built. Can't you see that? But this way, with Sally to believe in me, and enough money to live comfortably, to go places, see things—well, you wait. Watch my smoke."

Oddly enough, she did believe him. And less than five years proved him right; less than five years from that bitter January evening Jimmy Bates would be able to support himself and Sally and the two round rosy babies . . . without Sally's money. "A new star," the critics would say, "has dawned in the literary heavens."

But that was almost five years away.

He asked now, "Jill, you sure you're all right?"

She said steadily, "I'm sure." She'd die before she'd ask Sally's husband for fifty dollars of Sally's money!

Sally came in with the pictures. Jill exclaimed over them, was dutifully thrilled; and at a little before eleven took her leave.

Sally kissed her good-bye. She said, "When I think if it hadn't been for you . . ."

Jimmy was at the door. Jill asked low,

"Are you happy, Sally?"

The younger girl clung to her a moment. She said breathlessly, "I'm so happy I could—cry."

"Don't," said Jill.

Downstairs Jimmy had the doorman call a taxi. He put a bill in the driver's hand. He took Jill's hand in his own. He said:

"So long, old-timer, I'll write you from abroad. At the old address." He added, still holding her hand, "Believe it or not, I've missed you."

"I've missed you too, Jimmy."

"How's Dan the Boy Wonder?"

"Still in South America . . . naturally."

He said, "You're in love with that guy. Don't say no, I'm Omar the Mind Reader. Being in love myself sharpens the perceptions. Take my advice—and the first boat. Pride's no good. I never had any and see where it landed me!"

She said, "You're a miserable worm. But—I do wish you happiness. Jimmy, if you aren't good to her—"

He said, "I'll take care of that. You don't have to tell me. Good-bye, stout fella."

The cars behind the taxi were honking. The doorman said something, the cab driver looked anxious. Jill climbed into the car with its smell of stale smoke and leather. She looked out and saw Jimmy standing on the curb, bare-headed, his hands in his pockets. She thought, driving toward Mrs. Larsen's, Well, I didn't get my fifty.

But somehow she believed in Jimmy. Jimmy and Sally would be—all right.

CHAPTER XV

By the middle of February Jill was very nearly desperate. She had procured a position as receptionist in a health institute and it had looked as if the job would be permanent. But unfortunately it wasn't altogether a health institute, as Jill soon found out. She had been so glad of the position, at twenty a week, it was easy work, sitting at a desk and making appointments. But the woman who ran the place was, it seemed, not licensed and various things went on behind closed doors of which Jill had no inkling although, she realized afterward, several of the girls employed there had tried to warn her.

The institute was raided, after a plain-clothes man had come there and made an appointment, and that was the end of it. Jill had been there less than a week and it was obvious to the men who questioned her that she knew nothing. So they let her go; and she was glad to go, grateful not to be forced to appear in court with the slim, hard-faced woman owner and the frightened, sullen girls. More than glad. But she did not get her money.

She had made the rounds of the steamship companies, right after leaving the Dennis house. All the hostess places were filled. Her first port of call had been the company which had once employed her. Not that she wanted to make the trip again, which would remind her of Dan. But it was a chance, they knew her there. The personnel woman had taken her address . . . just in case. "We're terribly busy," she said, "we're running the cruises as close together as we can. Travel has picked up a lot, you know, people book their passage 'way ahead."

Shortly after she had left the health institute the steamship line called her. Could she report for work tomorrow? Yes, a cruise. The hostess who had been on that boat all season had been taken to the hospital on reaching port yesterday . . . appendicitis. Would Jill care for the position, for one trip, at the most, perhaps two?

Would she care for it!

Not much money, very little money, but her passage, her meals, and a roof over her head. She hung up and flew to find Mrs. Larsen. She said, "I've got a cruise job."

"Then you'll be leaving me?"

"Yes. I'll be back. Of course I don't expect you to

keep the room. But—if you'd keep my things? I could pay a little, for storage."

Mrs. Larsen offered with unexpected generosity, "I'll keep them for nothing, Miss Hamilton. You've been a good lodger. Always paid your rent in advance and given me no trouble at all."

Thank heaven for the summery clothes which would do nicely on a South American cruise. It would be summer down there. And crossing the equator it would be hotter than the seven hinges. Jill packed her bag, repacked the trunk she would leave, left Mrs. Larsen a schedule of ports, and departed for the piers ahead of the passengers.

It was like coming home. For this was her boat. Hers and Dan's. She knew the captain, the purser, everybody. None had changed. And they seemed glad to see her back.

But after the first day or so it wasn't such fun. She kept remembering Dan. Here they had danced, here they had had tea together, there they had walked on deck, and here they had stood side by side looking down at moon-bright water, feeling the magic of moonlight running in their veins like silver blood.

She thought, I was a fool. He was right, I couldn't take it. What did it matter where he went, or what he had, if we were together?

She performed her duties meticulously but her heart

was not in them. Going down that other time she had amused the unattached young men, cautiously, but with a light heart, she had danced a lot, and had an amazingly good time. This trip she didn't seem to care. She had found nice unattached girls for the young men; she organized bridge games, fancy dress parties, little festivities, and interested herself in the passengers from a purely official standpoint.

But there was one old lady who was different.

She was traveling with a schoolteacher daughter, who was so busy studying Spanish that she had little time for her mother. Mrs. Watson was seventy-five, spry as a cricket, slim as a willow. She had the whitest hair in the world and it was curly. She had a little lined face, very blue eyes, and Jill fell in love with her the first day out.

She was with her as much of the time as possible. It so happened that they were together at the table. The daughter, when not immersed in Spanish, was seasick and kept to her cabin. Mrs. Watson said loyally:

"Emma hasn't been very well. Looks peaked. She took this vacation mostly on my account but she needed it worse. Put in a substitute, she did. She's always been saving. A good daughter."

Jill learned quite a lot about the old lady before the first week was over. She'd been born and bred in Vermont and when Jill asked where and Mrs. Watson told her, Jill cried, "But that's six miles from where I was born."

"Six miles? Where would that be?"

Jill told her, smiling, and Mrs. Watson said, "Hamilton. Hamilton. I thought you looked like him. I knew Lem Hamilton. We went to school together. You've got his red hair and there's something in the set of your shoulders . . ."

Lemuel Hamilton was Jill's grandfather. Jill remembered him, dimly.

Mrs. Watson said, "The world's such a small place. Lem's granddaughter. Tell me all about yourself."

Jill told, sketchily. Leaving home, believing she could sing on the radio, the disappointments, the struggles, the jobs. Mrs. Watson listened looking out at the blue water. The ship's engine throbbed steadily, the ship's brat ran past screaming—there is always a bad child on every cruise—pursued by a weary governess. The little Spanish woman who had been in the States on business, with three well-behaved but young children, passed with her brood and smiled at Jill and the old lady. The best-looking bachelor went by with the prettiest girl. They would be engaged before the ship docked in Manhattan again but—would it last?

"Seems as if," said the old lady mildly, "you don't stay put for long."

Jill tried to explain, her lack of training, the back-

260

water in which girls of her age had found themselves. "The kids who left school later than I did got all the breaks," she said.

Her little passenger nodded. She remarked after a moment:

"Restless. I've noticed that in young people your age. Lem was that way. Did you know he ran away, shipped before the mast, when he was still in school?"

"No," said Jill, "I didn't."

"Well, he did," said her friend. "Came back ten pounds lighter and a heap more experienced. I liked Lem at lot. If it hadn't been for Darius—"

"Darius?"

"Darius Watson. I married him," said Mrs. Watson simply, "and we went to Iowa. It wasn't much of a country in those days. I mean, it wasn't as settled. Darius was a carpenter builder. We made out. We had a funny little house and a lot of land . . . and the three children were born out there. Two died. The other one lived to grow up. He died in the war. Then after we come back East, Emma was born."

Jill said, "A real pioneer."

"I never thought of it like that. My people were," said Mrs. Watson, "back in the old days. My father, he was a country doctor. You don't know what pioneering is till you've been married to a country doctor in New England, seventy-five years ago. Many's the time my mother traveled ten-fifteen miles by sleigh in winter or horseback in summer, and helped a baby into this world, or sat by the dying. She made up my father's prescriptions, she went out and got herbs. She was a pioneer . . . they all were in those days. Your grandfather too. Bought him a hard piece of land, gentled it under the plow. You should be proud of your blood, Jill; it's good blood, strong, there's courage in it. Sometimes I think if the young people today had less cheap pleasure and more expensive hardship the world would be a lot safer for them and their children."

They talked a great deal during the trip down. And when the ports were reached, Jill usually found herself ashore with Mrs. Watson and with Emma, who was a vague, spare woman, very pleasant, but utterly absorbed in herself. "Emma," said Mrs. Watson, sighing, "is a good girl but she don't laugh much."

Jill and Mrs. Watson laughed often. Everything was new to the old lady and she adored it. She loved the strange, sun-baked towns, the dark faces, the beggars, the old churches. She loved everything. She had the candid, unspoiled heart of a child, and she enjoyed every moment.

"Always wanted to travel," she said, "and it's never too late. Got my eyesight, my hearing, and a good digestion, thank Providence, and I can beat Emma sight-seeing."

"You can beat me too," said Jill, worn out from a day ashore with the indefatigable old lady.

One night, having found a fourth for several bridge games and gone over the plans for a ship's treasure hunt with the purser, Jill came up on deck and looked for Mrs. Watson. She found her lying back in a chair, looking at the great tropical stars. Emma was nowhere to be seen.

"Mind if I sit down?"

"Do, I was waiting for you. Take Emma's chair. She's writing letters. All she does is write letters. The two days we were in Bermuda she sent forty postals."

Jill said absently, "I suppose so . . ."

The old lady said:

"You weren't listening. Something on your mind?"

"Yes," said Jill, "I was thinking . . . of my last trip."

"Man?" asked her friend shrewdly.

"No. Yes. Oh, of course," said Jill, "isn't it always a man?"

"What happened to him?"

"He's down here . . . in the interior," Jill answered.

"You going to join him?" began the old lady. "So that's why you haven't paid any attention to all these young spriggins aboard. When? Where? I'd like to give you a wedding present."

Jill said, "No, I'm just hostess on this cruise to Buenos Aires and back, with stopovers," she said, "at Bermuda, Rio, Santos, Montevideo."

"And excursions," added the old lady raptly. "I'll never forget riding on that cogwheel train to Corcovado. Tell me about your young man."

Jill said, "He's tall . . . he's an engineer . . . he wanted me to marry him and live down here with him."

"And you wouldn't?"

"No."

"Why?"

"I had a good job," Jill told her, "and I thought . . . Well, Dan had a chance at a job in New York, with a fine salary and a future. He didn't take it. It was the sort of work he didn't like. He likes to be in crazy places working his head off for very little money, getting fevers and running into danger."

"And you," asked the old lady gently, "wouldn't like that?"

"No," said Jill, "of course not."

Mrs. Watson sighed. She said, "Times have changed since a woman went where her man's work was, and worked with him and for him and bore his children and didn't think she was sacrificing anything, because she knew she wasn't. I don't know what's wrong with this world. It isn't the depression. We've had depressions before . . . maybe they didn't last as long, maybe they weren't as hard . . . but then in the old days we weren't used to as much as now. It all evens up. Look at the papers, men killing themselves, women going crazy, because they lose money, jobs. People didn't do those things in the old days. They had too much self-respect. A bank failed and a man tightened his belt and a woman saw to it that she didn't spend more than he made. And all this business about getting married and keeping your job if you're a woman and not letting your husband have the feeling which every man wants to have, that he's head of things, that he does the providing. Sometimes I think people are crazy, too many automobiles, radios, airplanes, fast trains, movie theaters. We didn't have many pleasures when I was a girl . . . a church social and picnics, concerts, and a traveling show or circus now and then. But we enjoyed them. I don't think people know how to enjoy things these days. Tell me what happened to you and this young man of yours."

Somehow Jill found herself telling all the hard times, the excitement, the Dennis job, everything. It was good for once to be able to pour out her heart as she hadn't to anyone, not even to Helen Elliott. And Mrs. Watson listened and sighed.

She said, "You're a stubborn little thing."

"Is that all you have to say?" asked Jill, with a choky sort of laugh.

"That's all. You don't deserve a man like that. He'd take care of you. You'd take care of him, in your way. That's what marriage was meant for. Two people, against the world. Where'd you say he is?"

Jill said, "I don't know much about it. It's inland from São Paulo . . . quite a trip."

Mrs. Watson said, "That little Sanchez woman is getting off at Santos. She's going to São Paulo by motor and stage and then she has to travel inland too, she was telling me. Poor little thing, she isn't awfully well. Might need a hand with the children."

Jill cried, "Are you trying to tell me to jump ship?"

"Mercy, no," denied Mrs. Watson. "I'm not trying to tell you anything. I know better than that, I was just figuring what I'd do if I were twenty odd again and loved a good man and had quarreled with him and let him go to a strange place all alone and came by chance within hailing distance of that place. Well, I must get to bed. Emma will be out for me in a little while and she'll scold."

Jill walked to her cabin with her. She stood there in the corridor feeling the sway and pitch, the pulse of the ship under her feet. She said wistfully:

"I know you think . . . Well, I don't know what

266

you think. But suppose he doesn't want me any more, Mrs. Watson. Suppose he thought that just because . . . I'd lost my good job . . . I'd taken second best?"

"When you put your arms around him," said Mrs. Watson, "he won't think that. Not for long. But I'm not giving any advice. Young folks don't want advice. All they want is to be told that what they intend to do is the right thing, and I haven't any idea what you intend to do."

She put her cool withered cheek against Jill's, kissed her with dry old lips. But the blue eyes were very young. She said, "Seems as if you had been taking all kinds of chances for seven years. Now when you have a chance to take a really good chance—"

Her door closed behind her.

Next day they were in Santos. There were side trips, to bathing beaches, Monte Serrat, Guaruja. In the afternoon the tourists would rejoin their ship, steam down the Santos River and head for the sea and Montevideo.

When the rumor ran through the ship that Jill Hamilton, the pretty redheaded hostess, had not returned and in the excitement of re-embarking some official slip had been made and her absence was not noticed until the ship was under way, Emma Watson hurried down to the cabin she shared with her mother, to tell her the news. She said, "She was with us at São Paulo. I thought she came back in the other car. I wonder what can have happened. I never trusted that girl, anyway."

"Because she has red hair?" asked Mrs. Watson, smiling.

"Don't be silly, mother. No; on general principles. I understand the purser is wild. And the captain. People are wondering," said Emma in a little whisper, "if she was kidnaped."

"I doubt it," said her mother calmly and settled the lace collar of her best silk frock.

"Mother! Do you know anything about this?"

"Why, of course not, Emma," replied Mrs. Watson mildly. "Why should I? But I'm sure nothing has happened to her. She's a very nice little girl. I hope," she added, as if to herself, "that she writes and tells me all about it."

Emma said slowly, "I believe you do know something."

Jill was at the American consulate talking to a young man. She was saying, "I know . . . it doesn't admit of any explanation . . . but . . ." She raised her eyes and the young man smiled, being susceptible. "You see, we quarreled. He hasn't the least idea . . . I thought . . . Oh, if I'd stopped to think I wouldn't have done it . . . but I thought . . . if I just *went* there . . ."

The young man was unhappy. He read things to her out of a book . . . relative to passports, vaccination, health certificates, identity books, photographs, and the certificate of good conduct which was required by the government from all women traveling alone. And, in the case of women traveling to be married, a Bond of Guarantee which should be produced by the happy fiancée, certified by the police, and the documents of authorization.

She said miserably, "I never thought about that."

The young man said, "I'll talk to the consul." He leaned back at his desk and looked at her. He said, "I happen to know one of the big shots here rather well." He blushed faintly. He was a fair young man who was in the process of courting, ceremoniously, the daughter of one of the official bigwigs in São Paulo. But he was still susceptible.

Jill said eagerly, "There's Mrs. Sanchez. She was on our boat. She's going from here into the interior, with her children. I'm sure she'd let me go with her. I could help take care of them, work my way."

"Have you," he asked her, "any money?"

"Not much."

Mr. Elgin shook his head. He said, "That's too bad too." He opened a desk and took out a wallet. He said, "I don't know why I'm doing this. Well, you're an American girl. If you have enough money to prove you aren't indigent, I may be able to wangle the necessary papers. We'll see. You can repay me . . . I may have to keep you here and notify your Mr. Hardy and then when he comes . . ."

She said, "Oh, that would be . . . No, please, please try to get me to him. . . . I mean, I'll go crazy waiting here."

She stayed a long time in the office. Mr. Elgin departed and returned to say that the consul wished to see her.

Jill came out of his office a half an hour later. It was evident that she had been crying. Her consul had been kind to her, and very gentle. But he hadn't approved. His duty was to send her to rejoin her ship. But under the circumstances . . . Well, he would get in touch with Mr. Hardy, and in the meantime he would see that she was taken care of, but if Mr. Hardy declined the responsibility . . .

It occurred to Jill that perhaps he might. That was when she had cried, to her everlasting shame.

The consul regarding her thought that Mr. Hardy would be a born idiot if he did anything so abnormal.

Should however Mr. Hardy signify his intention to wed, then the consul was sure that the necessary papers could be obtained, the red tape cut, and that Jill could be married in the consulate.

She left No. 51 Rua Livero Badaro under the escort of Mr. Elgin, who took her to the hotel in which Mrs. Sanchez was stopping. At the Esplanada, Mrs. Sanchez, whose English was good and whose heart was kind, welcomed her. She would be, she said, after the story had been told, very glad of Jill's company and help. She would have to wait for several days in São Paulo until her husband and sister joined her. She added that if Jill was willing she could share a room with the older girls and in that way save expense.

So it was arranged. Jill, lying awake through the hot night, was cold and feverish by turns. What had she done? Mr. Elgin would notify the boat of course where she was . . . and why. If Dan did not come to São Paulo for her, if she had to be sent to a port like a convict—she wondered if she would go in chains—to rejoin her ship, she felt that she would never hold up her head again.

She waited four days. For three of them she had Mrs. Sanchez for company and the dark, well-behaved children. She went sightseeing with them, reporting dutifully twice a day at the Rua Livero Badaro. She took the children to see the largest concrete building in the world, or rather they took her, as they had been there many times before . . . this was the Matinelli Building, twenty-five stories high. She walked with them in the Jardin da Luz and through the municipal market. She went with them to the movies. And waited.

During this time she learned something about the

transport problem of Brazil . . . she learned that the interior was cut off from the coast, except in the north, by high mountains and that the present trend was toward road building rather than railways. Mr. Elgin, who had been born in Brazil of American parents, shook his head. He said:

"Railways, eh? I don't envy your boy friend his job!"

On the fourth day Mrs. Sanchez kissed her tearfully, exclaimed over the romantic circumstances which had thrown them together, and left with her darkly handsome husband, her astonishingly blond sister, and the children. And on the fifth day, as Jill sat in the outer office of the consulate, Dan walked in.

He was very lean, very brown, and his clothes were more or less nondescript. She went from red to white as she saw him and her heart pounded in her ears and she felt sick and thought, I won't faint, I've never fainted . . . it would be too absurd.

He said, "Jill!" and strode toward her and she spoke his name and there was a singing blackness.

When she came to she was in a quiet room on a couch, with the electric fans going. Dan was sitting beside her and her hair and face were drenched with water.

He said, "It's all right, darling."

Jill sat up shakily. She told him, "I was—just *scared*.

Scared you wouldn't have me. Scared I'd have to rejoin the ship."

He said tenderly, "You are an idiot. If you'd let me know you were on your way . . ."

She told him, "Dan, how did I know you'd still want me?"

He leaned over, caught her in his arms, and kissed her. He said, "I'll want you—always—all my life. But to come down like this . . . they tell me you jumped ship!"

"Dan, I did! Wasn't it outrageous?"

He laughed. "It was marvelous," he said. He kissed her again. "Works her way down," he said, "jumps ship."

She thought, he believes it was in my mind from the first. Well, she told herself, closing her eyes, there's no need to disillusion him . . . and perhaps he's right.

"It's been so long," he told her, "and I wondered. What happened, did you get fed up at the Dennises and," he asked her, "see the error of your ways?"

She said evasively, "Jimmy and Sally eloped, Dan, and of course I wasn't needed any more."

"Eloped! Well, of all—"

Mr. Elgin came in. He said, "The chief will see you now. Think we'll have things fixed up pretty soon."

"Better," Dan said rising, "I've got to get back on the job."

At the door of the office he paused and looked down at Jill. He warned her anxiously, "It's no bed of roses, darling. Heat and natives, dust and hard work, and being lonely. Sure you aren't afraid?"

She said clearly, "I'll never be afraid any more, Dan, as long as we're together."

The door opened and they stepped through to whatever future awaited them. And Jill thought, holding Dan's hand, Well, it's a new job—and this time it's permanent.

(If you have liked this story you will enjoy reading FAITH BALDWIN'S *last book*

HOTEL HOSTESS)

CHAPTER I

MISS MANHATTAN had scrubbed her face and put on her best frock, for spring, her seasonal guest, had come to town. The steel and stone towers aspired to a cleaner blue sky and the warm May sunshine was like a celestial smile. The parks were green, the shrubs had blossomed, the hotel window boxes were gay with flowers. Tulips marched in pink and white rows around the Plaza fountain and walking along Fifth Avenue you saw more pretty girls than you had ever seen in all your life.

One of the prettiest was riding uptown on the top of an open bus. Her name was Judith Gillmore and, as she was a natural redhead with black eyes and a spectacular figure, more than one gentleman occupying space near by stole appreciative glances at her, moved by the influence of the superbly silly season and the evidence of his own eyes. But Judith was, or appeared to be, oblivious of silent admiration, clearing of throats and straightening of neckties. She was engaged in doing something which no pretty girl in her senses should be doing on a bright May morning. She was indulging in mathematics. She had a notebook and a little pencil and she was methodically setting down figures and adding them up. The sum total did not seem to please her. She drew her fine dark brows together and tapped a small narrow foot with impatience.

The bus slowed to a stop and a girl walking along the Avenue glanced up for no particular reason. But seeing Judith, she stopped in her tracks and shouted. She had a clear and carrying voice.

"Judy! Judy Gillmore!"

Judith jumped and looked down. Then she waved and made frantic gestures.

"Polly!" she called.

"Get off!" yelled Polly with determination.

"Get on!" suggested Judith.

By this time the passengers were much amused, and the bus had started forward slowly.

Polly Andrews was running along beside it, to the disgust of irate taxi drivers.

"Got a lunch date?" she howled, and every man on top of the bus pricked up his ears.

"No," shrieked Judith.

"Then get off at the next corner and wait," suggested Polly, screaming.

Laughing, flushing a little, Judith pressed the signal button and rose to make her way to the stairs. When the corner was reached and the amused conductor had helped her off, she crossed to the curb and stood there waiting. In a few minutes Polly joined her and they fell into each other's arms with the exuberance of two old friends who have not seen each other for a long time.

"Well, I'll be a so-and-so," said Polly affectionately, "you look like the Federal debt! But more than a billion, my dear, more than a billion. Let's go somewhere and eat like anything and talk like mad. Am I glad to see you, or am I?"

Judith said, smiling:

"You're looking very fit yourself. I'd love to have lunch with you, Polly, if you're sure—"

"Of course I'm sure," said Polly.

"I have to catch a train," Judith told her, "but not until late afternoon."

"Then come along," said Polly, "and make it snappy. I'm dying to hear all about you. Do you realize that we haven't seen each other for four years? Since, in fact, we modestly received the plaudits of the throng upon graduating from dear Miss Manners, back in the old days."

"Is it only four years?" asked Judith, with a sort of mild wonder.

LIN 10-83
SRSS 4-84
WC 8-84
CST 10-84
SJR 11-84
Fre 1-87
Dav 5-87
MAR 6/95
9-15-97   8-3-98   32 T